The JAR
and
PINEAPPLE

LESLEY SAINTY

The Jar and Pineapple

Copyright © 2023 Lesley Sainty

The moral rights of the author have been asserted.

Prominent people from the period are characterised to add historical context to this novel. Most dialogue and narrative accredited to these historical figures is purely fictitious. No judgement or comment of any kind is implied nor intended.

Cover design and formatting www.jdsmith-design.com

Published by Lesley Sainty

All enquiries to yourcreativemediauk@gmail.com

ISBN: 9798860286511 (paperback)

First published, 2023

Cheltenham, May 1834

Chapter 1

Hammering rain drowned out the sound of the man's footsteps as he turned off the high street into a narrow passage. It had been a wet May, but the air was warm, even at midnight. Once inside the dark entrance he paused for a moment, his breathing heavy. Tall buildings now surrounded him and sheltered him from most of the rain apart from a steady dripping, and he drew his threadbare coat to his ears and tipped his cloth hat further over his face.

The man moved deeper into the blackness; his footsteps echoing in the quiet passage before he came to a stop, turned, and then looked back at the entrance. The light from the street silhouetted a tall male form; its face shadowed by a top hat. Suddenly, the figure moved quickly down the passage and grabbed the waiting man's arm to lead him wordlessly further down the alleyway. The passage smelt damp and sour as the tall man leaned forward, bringing his mouth close to the other man's ear; his lips touching his cloth hat.

'Have you destroyed my note?' the tall man's voice was deep and resonant.

'Aye, when do I get me dues?'

'When you have delivered.'

'Tha' I'm already workin' on, you understand? We have to wait.'

The tall man stood back, slipped a folded piece of paper from the pocket of his greatcoat, and thrust it into the rough hand of the waiting man before leaning menacingly close once more. 'You know how I work. You will be paid handsomely once the job is done,' he snarled. 'Now take this. It has full instructions. It must work, no matter what. He must be stopped.'

The waiting man grunted, turned, and shoved the note deep into his pocket. He tugged his hat even further over his face and stumbled up the alleyway out of the darkness, sighing heavily as he was united with the weak light filtering from the inns and hotels on the high street.

The tall man paused in the passage, took one look over his shoulder at the light entrance before looking keenly into the blackness and striding off further into the gloom.

Chapter 2

The band had started its morning performance under the canopy of the Montpellier Spa, and though the weather was wet, there was a fair sprinkling of people on the promenades. Visitors to the pump room inside the long-pillared building of Cotswold stone had taken their morning waters before embarking on a walk: ladies in groups wearing their finest; elderly couples arm-in-arm pacing the promenade, and men in pairs observing the scene. The ten-strong orchestra proudly wore new uniforms for the opening of the season: dark blue frock coats; officers' caps trimmed with a broad silver band, and a white silk tassel and crimson sash. They played a lively march as they prepared for the start of the upcoming evening promenades.

The arrival lists published in the weekly editions of the Looker-On's society pages afforded evidence of the increasing reputation of Cheltenham. The town lay in a beautiful natural bowl, surrounded by lofty hills, and its eminence as a spa town in which to take the healing waters was well-established. And yet, Cheltenham had gained a reputation as a hedonistic and self-gratifying place - a place which attracted pleasure-seekers during the season, especially during the three-day horse race meeting in July.

Here at the gently sloping Montpellier Grand Promenade, a walk which connected the popular spa to the glass-topped

Montpellier Arcade, visitors browsed for trifles in the shops now housed in a terrace of three-storey buildings. Beyond this stretched Cheltenham's tree-lined Well Walk, which meandered past the famous Royal Old Well, over a pretty bridge crossing the River Chelt and onto St Mary's Church in the distance.

At the top of the promenade, a grand blue carriage came to a sudden stop. A hand gloved in pale blue rested on the carriage window, and a face with fine features and dark brown eyes appeared, gazing out at a new boutique. Actress Maria Mount had returned to Cheltenham for the season. Before the carriage driver could jump down to open the door, she had placed a pale blue bonnet over her raven curls, lifted her white linen dress and stepped daintily out onto the gravelled walkway. She crossed the promenade, reaching the window of Madame St-Ange's where a large poster advertised 'New Spring Fashions from Paris.'

Peering into the window, Maria smiled, showing two pinpoint dimples in her rosy cheeks. She was a voluptuous beauty: her hair was curled into ringlets and her eyes sparkled as she beckoned to her maid, who had hurriedly followed her out of the carriage. The actress pointed to a long Grecian-style gown in the window, its style replicating the sculpted attire of the statues of armless ladies which graced the entrances to the shops. The white-painted, heavy-robed caryatid sculptures, resembling the classical models on the Acropolis in Athens, lined the whole walk supporting the stepped cornices.

Gazing up and down the Grand Promenade, Maria turned to her maid and in a low, musical voice, asked, 'Oh, but all these changes! Did you know Hetty?'

Hetty smiled, 'Not at all, miss. Being in London all these months, I'm sure there is much we don't know about.'

Maria looked further down the promenade. Other visitors had paused to stare, both at the actress and the grand carriage, whispering behind gloves, but she was too absorbed by the scene to notice and began to move gracefully along, peering curiously into the various shops. Next to the boutique a new medical and chemical repertory displayed colourful jars and potions promoting 'miracle' cures for all ills. Maria saw other traders new to Montpellier; there was a butcher with a myriad of meats hanging up, both in the window and inside the shop. A portly greengrocer stood proudly on a doorstep next to his fine display of bright fruits and vegetables, his thumbs tucked into the straps of his striped apron. He nodded and tapped his hat at Maria and her maid, who returned his greeting.

'Well, I must say it has all happened rather quickly... and this...' Maria came to a stop and gasped.

Taking pride of place in the centre of this new set of shops was a confectioner's, the front of which was a delight to behold. There was a dark green sign above the shop bearing curly gold letters which read 'The Jar and Pineapple.' Painted next to the name was a gold pineapple. Another sign hanging from the building showed the same exotic fruit but larger. Below the signs, two large bay windows displayed rows of shelves filled with jars of all shapes and sizes. Inside each jar multi-coloured treats were stored: orange barley sugars in a squat glass jar next to pastel-coated liquorice in a tall one; violet-hued icing sugar drops packed another, competing with a neighbouring jar filled to the brim with pineapple squares.

Maria clapped her hands and laughed with delight as she took in the luxury before her. Hetty stood wide-eyed. The door of the shop was enticingly ajar, and they sniffed the air: the scent of violets, orange flowers, jasmine roses and elder flowers drifted from inside. On one side of the bay window a small paper sign advertised 'Mr Bonfils from France... A confectioner in the business of making English, French, and Italian wet and dry sweetmeats and ices.' Maria and Hetty shared a glance and hurried through the door.

Inside The Jar and Pineapple, the experience was even more sensory and overwhelming. The delightful floral smell increased and was combined with an almost tangible warmth in which you could taste the sweetness. Round, delicate iron tables with marbled tops, and wrought-iron chairs adorned with pastel-coloured cushions were assembled across a black-and-white chequered floor. Matching pastel walls depicted scenes from Paris and Montpellier: street scenes and copies of the Grand Tour paintings. Covering most of the back wall of the large square room was a long copper counter with glossy dark green tiles underneath. Behind the counter, the confectioner displayed the tools of his craft. His equipment for refining sugar resembled that of a foundry, with specialised pans for melting, devices that calibrated heating and cooling, and a variety of moulds to create shapes for chilled custards and ice cream, frozen mousses, jellied fruit, candies, and caramels.

Standing behind this counter wearing a pristine white apron, was a small, slight man with black hair parted in the middle, a thin moustache, and a wide smile. He swept his arms up as Maria and Hetty walked in. 'Welcome *mesdames!*'

Mr Bonfils was new to Cheltenham, like so many other shopkeepers who had seen the potential of promoting their quality and luxury goods to the visitors who promenaded the walks. Trained in Paris and then London, his art required as much precision as a sculptor or silversmith. All morning, his delicate hands had been busy directing his staff who filled buckets with ice and salt, scraped and stirred pots, and tended to freezing mixtures in the bustling backroom. Now, front-of-house waiters in pristine white coats proudly served the luxury ices, fruits, creams, custards, and multitudes of sweets and candies to wide-eyed rich customers, who had never seen such specialities.

Maria and Hetty approached the counter, in awe of their host. The other customers, including two ladies sitting near the counter, looked on in amazement.

'Mr Bonfils? What a pleasure! Maria Mount.' The actress put out a hand.

Without a pause or any acknowledgement of her fame, Mr Bonfils nodded, took Maria's hand and bowed to her and then to Hetty. He picked up a small bowl from the counter with both hands and placed it in front of them. It was filled with pebble-like violet sweets. 'Now, ladies, these have been made from the finest of ingredients, including petals picked by my own hands from the *Jardin des Plantes* in Paris. Now try!'

Maria and her maid looked at each other, smiled and took a violet drop each. The smooth, hard outer shells made a tapping sound as they rolled them round their mouths. Maria went quiet as she savoured the sweetness. She momentarily reached for a silver locket around her neck and stroked it gently between her fingers as she bit into the sweet drop, which dissolved its delicate flavour onto her tongue. Coming out of the daze, she exclaimed,

'My goodness, Mr Bonfils, these are delicious. What a treat to have you here!'

'*Madame*, it is my pleasure.' The confectioner beamed and bowed. 'And you must try my ice creams. I have made a special batch just now.' He waved his arms flamboyantly towards the ladies near the counter. Maria looked over her shoulder and nodded kindly at the two ladies, who were still gazing at her, with untouched ices in front of them. Maria turned back to Mr Bonfils.

'I'm afraid Hetty and I must be getting on, but I will certainly return to try your ices, Mr Bonfils. I promise you that.'

Maria offered her hand again and bowed to the confectioner before turning swiftly and walking out of the shop to her waiting carriage, Hetty following closely behind.

The two ladies with ices, who had been watching the whole encounter in shocked silence, now turned their attention back to the delicate glass bowls in front of them. They were filled with peach-coloured ice bombes: spheres of frosted ice impressed with little peaches, topped with yellow flowers.

The lady with blonde curls stared at her friend opposite,

who had already started to scoop the ice cream into her mouth with a dainty spoon.

'Did you not notice who just walked in?'

'Yes, I did, but, oh, you really should try this one,' her friend murmured.

'And have you heard she is to be performing in *Romeo and Juliet* at the Cambray Theatre? She has become quite the successful actress since her last visit to Cheltenham.'

Her friend nodded and continued to enjoy her peach bombe.

The blonde lady giggled, 'No doubt a few of her admirers will be returning to town. Colonel Buckley will be here, of course, and what with the races returning too. Isn't she just as beautiful close up? We must go and watch her. Oh, we must!'

Her friend put down her spoon, looked around furtively, took off her glove, swiped the bowl with her finger and licked it.

'Oh, yes, we must,' she agreed.

Overhearing, Mr Bonfils came to a halt in his sweet-making orchestra and looked over from behind the counter. 'Maria Mount? She is an actress? Well, I…' He shook his head slowly and smiled. 'And the races, I hear? I have been reading about them in the *Cheltenham Chronicle*. Ladies, do tell me all.' He leaned across the counter so his face was level with his seated customers. The ladies looked at each other for a moment, delighted at the attention.

Mr Bonfils laughed and tapped his nose. 'Ladies, I can assure you that The Jar and Pineapple will soon be the only place to go for all the latest gossip.'

The blonde lady raised her eyebrows. 'Oh there is much to find out about. Mr Bonfils. It all happens here in Cheltenham. For a start, we are the centre of the fashionable world for a few days when the annual races take place.' She paused, considering. 'I think the race organisers are very brave to be venturing back into Cheltenham after being forced out. You must have heard about the Reverend Cole?' She turned to her friend and nodded vigorously. 'I hear he already has a sermon planned for this coming Sunday.'

Mr Bonfils put a sugared hand on his chin. 'I have heard about the reverend, and I read something he wrote in the paper. I cannot remember what about, but I do recall he sounded like a very determined man. Tell me more, *madame*.'

The blonde lady delighted at the gossip. 'Determined is the word. He has been set against the races and everything and everyone associated with them since his arrival in Cheltenham, oh, over seven years ago now. He is even against the theatre. One would have thought he might have mellowed after his marriage and subsequent fatherhood, but no, not at all.'

'Oh, not at all!' her friend chipped in. 'He is just as determined as ever. I will be very interested to see what happens now the races are returning. I can imagine that neither the reverend nor his followers are taking it well. I am even tempted to go to his sermon on Sunday.'

Mr Bonfils smiled and nodded before straightening up. He smoothed his white apron and beamed as another two ladies entered the shop. 'Excuse me, *mesdames*,' he said, as he turned to greet his new customers.

Chapter 3

The weather had brightened and the walks to the parish church of St Mary's were dry and pleasant. The trees on each side of the walks were thickly planted and cut to form an arch impenetrable by the rays of the sun and by any but continued heavy rain.

This Sunday morning at St Mary's, the congregation had gathered in great anticipation to hear the Reverend Francis Cole's 'Sermon for the New Season', and latecomers found they could hardly get in for the crowd. They waited patiently in the churchyard as the queue moved slowly into the church: a squat building with a conical spire. The golden Cotswold stone glowed in the sunlight and the rustling lime trees surrounding the church accompanied a joyful ringing of bells which served as a call to the faithful.

Amongst those waiting were families with children dressed smartly in their best suits, smocks, and shoes; couples young and old peered eagerly around while larger groups leaned in. Further back, some unaccompanied gentlemen stood apart from the crowd, waiting to dart in at the last minute. Unnoticed, an ill-shaven man with a threadbare coat and cloth hat stood far away near a lime tree and watched as the procession dutifully entered the church. At the last moment, he merged into the crowd.

Inside St Mary's, the organ played solemnly as the congregation settled into their rented seats or moved to stand in the aisles. Couples sat with their heads bent close together and mothers put fingers to their lips to hush children while fathers gazed up at the galleries which extended around the inner interior of the ancient church to allow three-tiered seating. People shuffled along the narrow tiers, eager to get a seat, however uncomfortable. Sunlight danced through the vast stained-glass windows at the front of the building, and soon the pews and aisles and even the porches were full of people who chattered and looked around. The lone man was one of the last to enter. He hovered by the door, hidden slightly by a pillar.

'Sit still now, make father proud.' A little girl with brown curls and a neat brown bonnet whispered, putting her hand on her smaller brother's knee. Beside them, their mother, a slight woman with the same brown curls and neat bonnet as her daughter smiled down at her children. Elizabeth Cole, the reverend's wife, habitually attended all three of her husband's Sunday services. Glancing behind her, she saw a trio of ladies on the opposite side of the church staring over. Elizabeth smiled and nodded to them, and they smiled back. She was used to this attention now and felt proud of the awe and respect she had gained since marrying the reverend.

Elizabeth felt the air of anticipation as the crowd waited, the sound of parents hushing restless children echoing in the cavernous space. Suddenly there was stillness and silence as two wooden doors at the back of the church opened.

The Reverend Francis Cole strode out into the church, along the aisle, and climbed the stairs to his raised pulpit. Those who were seated rose in unison and, although there was complete quiet, people still shuffled and craned their necks to gain a first glimpse. Dust danced in the sunlight as the quiet lasted and Cole stood in the pulpit. His usually friendly and handsome face now held a sense of foreboding. His eyes were fixed, and his mouth was pursed as if in anger. Elizabeth kept her eyes on him, and she felt a thrill of excitement. Even though he was now her husband, she often felt in awe of him. Having been one of his devoted followers for many years, she still pinched herself at the idea that he now belonged to her.

Cole methodically removed a pair of black kid gloves, reached for his gold rimmed spectacles which were dangling from a chain around his neck, and placed them on his nose. He then opened his large leather-bound bible very deliberately and unfolded some notes inside. Finally, he looked down at his congregation and in a very quiet, natural, and warm voice said, 'My brethren – please be seated.'

Elizabeth briefly tore her gaze from her husband to sit and check that her children were still and listening.

The reverend paused as the congregation settled down and then continued in a steady voice, 'I had intended for this service to be a happy and joyful one. As you will know, we will soon celebrate the opening of Cheltenham's Free Church in St Paul's, along with another new school. However, events force me to delay talk of these subjects to a later time. Word has reached me of the return of events which threaten the good works in this town and all its Godly inhabitants and, as before, I cannot and I dare not be silent.'

The reverend stared out at the rapt faces of the congregation. He dropped his glasses to his ample chest and stood back with his hands clasped before him. Elizabeth, keen to look behind her to see the enraptured faces of her husband's audience instead kept her eyes forward as his clear, deep voice now started to boom out across the church. 'Christian Brethren, I speak of the works of darkness.' The reverend paused again, and the congregation seemed to hold its breath. 'The annual Cheltenham Races are now approaching and while we succeeded in casting off these works of evil before, they, and all their associated revelry, are threatening to return to town.'

There was a murmuring as people looked around with wide eyes at those next to them. People knew the news already but wanted to hear what the reverend had to say. Elizabeth quickly glanced around. How he casts such a spell, she thought as she returned her gaze to her hands. She had been reading the *Cheltenham Chronicle* and the letters of both support and opposition to the races. Elizabeth admired her husband for taking on the landowners; the people who had ruled the town for so long. She knew about the attractions of the races, the spas, and the theatre - along with the celebrated return of actress Maria Mount. Elizabeth looked up and turned her attention back fully to the sermon.

The reverend's voice was quiet again and almost soothing as he gently rested his hands on the side of the pulpit and continued: 'But, my brethren, let us put on armour of light. Let us walk honestly as in the day, not in rioting and drunkenness, not in chambering and wantonness, not in strife and envying. I have said before: All who in any measure promote or participate in the races are partakers of their guilt and subject to their plagues. It is therefore the duty of every virtuous citizen, and every pious Christian, not only to come out from such things himself but to endeavour in every possible way to stem the torrent of vice.'

Nods and murmurs rippled through the congregation as the reverend raised his voice. Elizabeth's heart began to beat fast, and she placed her hands in her lap to steady them. Her children looked up at her and then at their father as he boomed, 'We tarry indeed in a world darkened with the sins of its inhabitants, but we must come out from them and be separate, we must not partake in their sins, or we will share their plagues. You cannot doubt what the works of darkness are? They are those which shun the light, and court concealment; those which men seek to hide from their fellows, and vainly try to conceal from God. They are pointed out to us more clearly in the words sensuality and malevolence. The apostle warns us against sensuality when he saith, "let us not walk in rioting and drunkenness in chambering and wantonness." These are works of darkness; and include, in the strong language of the original, every species of sensual gratification, from the most splendid scenes of fashionable dissipation and refined luxury, to the lowest grade of abominable licentiousness, and loathsome vice; both are abhorrent to the character of a Christian who is to keep himself unspotted from the world. Abstain from fleshly lusts which war against the soul.' The reverend was now stretching out his right arm and pointing his finger into the congregation. Some children whimpered but their parents hushed. The man by the door had now come out from behind the pillar and stood with his eyes fixed on the speaker, his face impassive.

The reverend continued, his eyes wide, 'Some seem to exist only to eat and drink; others to buy and sell and get gain and the fear of God is not before their eyes; therefore, they defraud and overreach one another and he is esteemed most highly who is most successful in the arts of deception. We know of many in Cheltenham who have chosen this path and continue to do so. Bewildered by present enjoyment or maddened by the vices of the flesh they run on to their own eternal ruin. Would to God that some of these might be awakened this year to a sense of their imminent peril! That they might commence another and a better course, before the shades of eternal night comes upon them, and their eyes are closed in the blackness of darkness forever!'

Oh, he is zealous, thought Elizabeth, but that is why I love him. She thought back to his arrival in Cheltenham and how she had quickly become one of his many admirers. Being both handsome and jovial, the reverend had succeeded in rapidly growing his flock to include many wealthy ladies of the town. He had persuaded some of them to not only support his worthy causes of charity schools for both boys and girls, but to donate sizable amounts of their fortunes. Elizabeth had been one of the less wealthy admirers and recalled making him a pair of embroidered slippers. He still wore those same slippers, now rather worn but a treasured symbol of their love for each other. Their marriage had caused some of the wealthy ladies of the congregation to be envious, however, most saw the union as a sign of the reverend's piety and personal disinterest in the material.

Now, the reverend bent forward over the pulpit cushion, as though he wanted to come down and into the very pews of his church, his voice measured. 'Now firmly to the races. Even though this sport has continued outside of our environs, its evil revelry spreads into the town. Now that it is returning even closer than before, we must not let its influence pervade our town again.' The reverend paused to turn over his notes and Elizabeth recalled the events of the races some years ago on Cleeve Hill when the grandstand was burned to the ground. Everyone suspected that the culprits were the reverend's more radical supporters, but she knew he had not condoned their actions. She shook her head slightly as the reverend continued, 'I have a firm conviction that the evils at which it points are as injurious to your temporal interests as they are destructive to your souls. The month preceding the race week is uniformly the least profitable to you, and that Cheltenham is less frequented at that period than during any other season of the year, cannot be denied. The races may benefit the few but they injure the many; they may attract those who generally speaking, are the least desirable visitors, but they deter others more numerous, more respectable, and who would tend to raise the character of the place, as well by their station in life as by their moral conduct. I leave the case in your hands, with a full conviction that the course of conduct which many will adopt, will be decidedly in favour of social order, morality, and religion.'

The reverend carefully closed his bible and stepped back. As if released from a spell, the whole church rose up and started to clap wildly; Elizabeth and the children among them. There were shouts from the porches to the farthest corners of the galleries of, 'We will do our duty!' and 'Down with the races!' The reverend looked at his wife and beamed. She nodded up at him and felt like she had never loved him more.

Now couples smiled at each other, smug in the knowledge that they had snubbed the races for years. Mothers nodded at their children sagely while fathers clapped sensibly or called out support. Children cheered in rapture at the chance to join in with the noise. All were united, except one. Unseen, the man in the threadbare coat near the door slowly turned, edged his way through the many people standing and walked out without a backward glance.

Chapter 4

The Cambray Theatre was housed in a tall, white-washed building in Cambray Place off the High Street. The back lane to the stage door was crowded with playgoers eager to see the celebrated Miss Mount who, this evening, would perform the lead role in a new showing of Romeo and Juliet. The actress's fame had grown since her last performance in Cheltenham three years previously. Whether this fame was due to her appearance at the renowned Covent Garden Theatre in London or because of her involvement with Gloucestershire's notorious Colonel William Buckley, only the gossips could speculate.

Today, the lane was almost blocked up with coaches, sedan chairs and a motley crowd on foot all jostling to get a space, while shouts of, 'She's here!' and 'It's her!' accompanied the sound of a grand blue carriage which rounded the corner and stopped at the entrance to the lane. There was a sudden hush amongst the crowd as the door to the vehicle opened and for a moment there was complete calm. The hills beyond the theatre that rose in various directions around the town were green and quiet in the still June evening.

The moment of quiet continued but people still shifted for space to watch as the door of the carriage opened. Hetty stepped out first; her cheeks were rosy, and her eyes darted over the crowd nervously as she waited on the carriage step. A footman hauled a brown case from the roof of the vehicle, stepped down and used the case to guide a path through the upturned faces. As footman and maid followed along the narrow path, there was a collective gasp as Maria Mount emerged from within the carriage. She put her gloved hand in the air and smiled. Maria's raven hair was curled into ringlets under a pale green bonnet and her brown eyes sparkled as she beamed at the crowd. The actress nodded and waved as she stepped down from the carriage, her other hand holding the back of her long green silk gown. A glimpse of her cream silk shoes and stockinet ankles caused another gasp among the crowd, then there was an excited murmuring and finally a cheer as Maria quickly made her way through the throng and into the narrow back door of the theatre. The actress gave a last look back and waved once more before the door closed and the on-lookers rushed to the entrance.

Inside the theatre, little else was heard but a din and bustle on the adjustment and regulation of places. The red velvet seats in the circles were filling up with finely dressed ladies and gentlemen while above, a great gas chandelier threw a dazzling light, illuminating the pit which was packed with those paying for cheaper tickets. Dressed less finely but still in their smartest suits and dresses they stood looking up and around at the scene. The ceiling featured a vast circular mural of blue and cream, edged with gold detail. The gold edge continued at the front of the stage and the arch above had a red velvet front, embroidered with fine gold thread. Around the sides of the auditorium were grand boxes two storeys high above the pit, furnished with the same red velvet and gold embroidered designs.

Watching the bustle from the dark corner of one of the grand boxes was Colonel William Buckley. A patron of the theatre, he was known to tread the boards on occasion and was welcomed enthusiastically whenever he chose to watch or perform at the Cambray Theatre. Being tall and well-built with roguish good looks and a swaggering confidence, Buckley could slip easily into the role of the hero in any play. This evening, however, he was firmly ensconced in the box and his heavy-set eyes were fixed on the stage. His fingers stroked his dark, generous sideburns and his strong jaw. His lips curled up into a slight smile.

Across the other side of the theatre from Buckley, in her own grand box, sat Lady Croft – an elegant woman in her early sixties with black hair elaborately curled and piled high on the crown of her head. The style was adorned with a fine black feather and her sparkling emerald earrings and necklace glittered in the light as she stood and leaned out over the side of the enclosure.

'Why is he not coming to sit with us?' Lady Croft asked her husband, waving a black-gloved hand in the direction of Buckley. As she watched with growing frustration, Buckley shifted further back into the darkness of his box, so all she could see was the bottom of his tailcoat and riding boots. Sitting beside her, his mouth hidden under his generous grey moustache, Lord Croft raised an uninterested eyebrow. 'My dear, if the good man chooses to sit alone this evening, then so be it.' He turned his face away as he muttered, 'It would do us all good to sit alone at times.'

'What was that my dear?' Lady Croft leaned towards her husband but quickly turned back again and beamed out into the auditorium when she noticed many of the well-to-do of Cheltenham observing her and the party she sat with.

Lady Croft eagerly turned to an equally elegant lady of similar age who stood near her at the edge of the box. Lady Glenfield's sparkling jewellery rivalled her companion's and her high eyebrows and cheekbones spoke of a grand beauty. Having had a few brief meetings at society events previously, Lady Croft was sure she would be more receptive to gossip than her husband as she ventured confidently, 'There are quite a few here to see our star performer tonight.'

'Oh, of course.' Lady Glenfield laughed and then turned away to look below, but as they sat down and waited for the audience to settle and the orchestra to strike up a note, she leant into Lady Croft. 'And you see who is here don't you?' Lady Glenfield's eyes darted across to the other side of the theatre.

Lady Croft shifted closer to her companion and then nodded in the direction of Buckley. 'You know she attracted the attention of William many years ago and that he solemnly vowed his intention to make her his wife? After all these years, it has still not happened. And yet, here he is tonight. Here to watch her no doubt.'

Lady Glenfield nodded and leaned in further.

'I blame his father for the way he is; of course he has a sizable fortune, but it is the title he wants.' Lady Croft explained, shaking her head.

'The Earldom? I thought as the eldest son, Colonel Buckley would naturally claim the title?' Lady Glenfield whispered.

'No he won't, much to William's shame. His parents were not officially married when he was born. The family has long contested that a private marriage had taken place prior to William's birth; so-called proofs were even taken to the House of Lords, but they were disallowed. His younger brother Craven, our new MP, is now entitled to the earldom. He was born after the Earl's official marriage, but has always refused the title.'

Lady Glenfield was now wide-eyed. 'Why?'

'Oh, to honour his older brother. Or perhaps he is scared of him? I don't really know, but claiming the Earldom has been William's quest since I have known him these past twenty years or more.'

'And is this why Buckley has never chosen a wife?'

Lady Croft gave her companion a knowing look and settled back into her seat.

By now, the whole audience was seated, and the orchestra had struck up a tune. The two ladies peered across at the opposite box where Buckley had emerged from the corner and brought his seat nearer to the side. In the box directly below and nearest to the stage, another man sat alone. Unlike Buckley, whose arms sprawled across the edge of the box, the young man sat upright with his arms folded patiently in his lap. His long nose gave him a haughty look as he tipped his head back to observe the stage and auditorium, and while he was not a particularly attractive man, he had a confidence in his bearing. He wore a well-tailored green frock coat over a white shirt with the collar neatly tied at the neck. A small gold ring on his little finger glinted as he briefly moved his hand to smooth his light brown curly hair.

Lady Croft's eyes darted from one man to the other then settled on the newcomer for a few moments before she turned back to Lady Glenfield and continued her gossip. 'Being an actor himself, William offered his services to perform at the benefit of Miss Mount all those years ago. The house was full to the ceiling they say, and Maria, of course, felt very grateful to him. They started their relationship then, and you must know she has since borne him two children?'

Lady Glenfield's eyes widened even further but she continued to nod while Lady Croft continued, 'How awful, can you imagine? I don't think many of Maria's fans know about her children. They are being brought up by family friends until William establishes his claim to the earldom. That's his excuse anyhow, but if you ask me, he has deluded the unfortunate girl for far too long. I keep telling him, but he will not listen.'

Lady Glenfield looked at her companion for a moment before turning her head back to the stage and shifting slightly away.

*

'Five minutes until curtain up, Miss Mount.'

Maria scrutinised her reflection in her dressing room mirror backstage. The circular looking glass was well-lit by gas lights on both sides and created a cosy glow in the small square space. The walls were painted red, and a small table placed in front of the mirror was strewn with pots of creams, feathers, and trinkets. The actress sat in a high-backed chair with scarves draped over it. A simple wardrobe stood in the corner of the room, and contained costumes stuffed inside while others spilled out onto the wooden floor. As usual, Maria had applied her own makeup; soft pinks and rosy cheeks made her look innocent, she thought. Her wide eyes belied her wisdom and resilience. She heard the excited chattering of the audience from beyond the dressing room – it was now time to pretend, she thought. If only they knew. 'Do I love this life?' Maria sighed softly to herself.

The actress looked away from the mirror to her large silver locket that she had carefully placed on the table beside her. Its clasp hanging open, the locket showed two painted miniature portraits: one of a brown-haired girl with big brown eyes and the other of a younger boy sharing the same features. Both children had rosy cheeks and were smiling out of the pictures. Under the custody of Buckley, Maria had been forced to give them up and stifled the yearning for her children by throwing herself into her performances. Maria sighed; brushed away a tear and looked towards the door. She took a deep breath and rose from her chair.

*

Back in the auditorium, the orchestra played as a man dressed in a black tailcoat entered the stage in front of the curtains. 'Welcome Ladies and gentlemen of Cheltenham! We promise you a special performance direct from the Covent Garden Theatre with the celebrated Miss Mount as Juliet and the esteemed Mr Hammond as Romeo. Following, there will be a performance of the very celebrated Mr de Egville from the

London Opera House performing the Grand Pas Seul casta-net dance of his own composition.'

The curtains parted across the stage and the audience gasped at a magical scene: the back wall had been painted with an expansive portrait of the Italian countryside; the fields terracotta and honey yellow against a pale blue sky. In stage front, a Mediterranean courtyard had been recreated with a rose-covered terrace. A balcony with steps was dressed with ivy and blossoming pink roses.

The play began with a dramatic fight between the Houses of Montague and Capulet: a market scene descended into chaos with shouting and swords flashing, while cabbages, carrots and potatoes flew across the stage to the delight of the audience. Buckley had sat back in his seat with a grin while the gentleman below lost his haughty look and assumed a multitude of expressions ranging from shock to pure delight as he laughed at every insult and sword blow. Those in the pit shouted and jeered.

After Mr Hammond's entrance as the love-sick Romeo, the whole auditorium gasped again in delight at the entrance of Maria Mount. She was wearing a simple, long, white dress with dusky pink waist sash. The actress's dark hair tumbled down her back as she swept across the stage and all movement and sound seemed to stop as she asked Lady Capulet in a soft husky voice,

'Madam, I am here. What is your will?'

Buckley leaned even further over in his box to view Maria on the stage, his face amused, while below, the young gen-tleman sat still and captivated at the actress's performance. Her Juliet was impassioned but tender and seductive. At no point did she catch the eye of Buckley, but twice she glanced at the young gentleman below who remained as still as he had been at the start of the performance. When it seemed Maria had looked his way, the young gentleman beamed back at the actress. Buckley frowned and briefly poked his head over the box to try and see who sat below.

As Juliet hurried off to Friar Lawrence's cell, the curtain fell for the interval and the audience erupted into applause and chatter. The young gentleman was the first up from his seat and out of the door of his box as the lights came up. At once, Lady Croft turned to Lady Glenfield. 'Oh, I do not know whether to watch the performance on the stage or the one that is going on opposite.'

Lord Croft raised his eyebrows. 'My dear, what could be more interesting than this wonderful performance?' He rose from his seat, stretched his arms behind his back, walked to the back of the box and motioned to a steward, who came hurrying over.

'Have you not been watching Buckley and the gentleman below him? Both captivated by Juliet, I tell you.' Lady Croft tutted. 'Find out who that gentleman is!' she called to her husband at the door, before turning back to Lady Glenfield, her eyes imploring.

'Have you noticed?'

Her companion grinned, 'Yes, I have. As fascinating as this performance is, I must agree that the faces of Buckley and the gentleman are just as enthralling.'

Lady Croft nodded, 'She has certainly not lost any of her famed beauty, I must say. No wonder she still has many admirers... but I imagine William would have something to say about that.'

Lord Croft had departed the box with the steward who now returned carrying a silver tray stacked with glasses of lemonade. As the refreshments were handed out, Lady Croft stood up and raised an inquisitive eyebrow at her husband who walked back into the box behind the steward.

'Yes, yes, I have my sources my dear. The young gentleman is a Mr Joseph Hayne of Staffordshire. A man of considerable wealth, or so I have just been reliably informed. Newly situated in Cheltenham I hear.'

Lady Croft clapped her hands in delight as she looked

back over the auditorium and then moved closer to the side of the box to peer over the edge.

'William has gone from his seat too!' she turned and looked at her companions, who laughed. 'Oh, I wonder what they are both up to! In pursuit of Miss Mount no doubt, but I am more interested now in the other gentleman. It seems as if William has some competition this evening.'

*

There was a knock at Maria's dressing room door as she put the final touches to her second outfit: instead of the floating white dress, she now wore a red velvet gown with a brown cape. Her heart skipped as she looked again at her reflection. A natural blush had risen on her cheeks as she expected to see the brooding face of Buckley, but instead her young assistant announced, 'A Mr Hayne desires to speak with you Madam. He was most insistent and said you would be expecting him.'

Maria sighed and she watched her face fall in the mirror before turning back and nodding to her assistant. I am not expecting anyone, she thought. She quickly shut the silver locket at her side and at once, the young man from the lower box entered the room. His haughty look had completely dissolved, and Maria recognised the simpering look worn by many of her admirers: a mixture of simple boyish awe and lust. He stood at the door, bowed, and held his top hat in his hands. His cheeks blushed and his eyes were bright, alert, and friendly.

'Mr Hayne? I believe you desired to speak to me and said I was expecting you?' Maria was polite but sat back in her chair and looked coolly at the young man.

He stared at the actress in startled wonder for a moment before clearing his throat. 'You must excuse my slight fib, but I was em...emboldened to approach you. Your performance has cast quite a spell over me and the audience this evening and...I had heard of your performances in London and was eager to meet you in person... Miss Mount.' The young man bowed.

Maria smiled kindly, 'I am flattered by your recognition Mr Hayne, but I do not wish to sound impolite – I must prepare for the second act.'

Joseph's eyes darted around the room as he shifted awkwardly from foot to foot.

'Ah, yes of course, please accept my apologies for the intrusion, but if I may be so bold, you must know of my ardent desire to see you again. I... I am new to Cheltenham and wondered if you would do me the honour of a promenade. I will send a formal invitation of course.' Joseph toyed with his hat and shuffled his feet.

Maria wondered at this man who she knew nothing of. He must have been younger than her, perhaps by three or four years. She looked him up and down and noticed his expensive attire and his neatness. She thought again of Buckley who had failed to call or even send a note since her arrival in Cheltenham. Her assistant at the door called, 'Five minutes Miss Mount.'

'Mr Hayne,' Maria met his gaze. 'This is certainly very forward of you, but I am flattered by your... informal invitation. Though I have many who ask to see me again, I will consider your offer. Please send a note to the theatre.' The young man bowed and looked to the ground as Maria turned back to her mirror. Before he could speak again, the assistant escorted him out of the dressing room.

*

In the main auditorium, a bell sounded and Lady Croft settled back into her seat. She turned to Lady Glenfield who once again leaned in as her companion launched back into gossiping.

'Miss Mount's background is quite understandable, of course you know? Her father was the manager of the Plymouth Theatre and her mother a much younger maid who for some reason became besotted with him. Of course, in country towns actors and actresses are looked down upon, so no respectable family paid Mrs Mount the least attention. Although the whole town was interested in her appearance, it regarded her simply with pity for marrying such an older man.'

'How do you know all of this Lady Croft?'

'Oh, I have eyes and ears all over the country,' Lady Croft beamed without any irony. 'Anyhow, the product of this union was Maria Mount, and she was brought up amid scenes little calculated to give her any self-respect, or a sense of propriety. She was on the stage at the tender age of 12 so they say. An interesting girl is in the jaws of ruin, who enters life as an actress, unless watched and protected by her family and friends.' Lady Croft frowned and narrowed her eyes.

As the lights went down for the second act, both of the gentlemen opposite had returned to their seats and were eagerly peering down onto the stage. The tragedy unfolded and with the demise of Miss Mount's Juliet in the penultimate scene, Mr Hayne wiped his eyes while Buckley yawned and looked at his pocket watch before narrowing his eyes at the stage, standing, and then walking out of his box.

'Well, he is surely coming to see us?' Lady Croft stood up, looked at her husband and peered over the side of the box again. The auditorium was a bustle and din as people went to relieve themselves or ventured to the bar for refreshment ahead of Mr de Egville's performance.

Lady Croft swung round as a voice boomed in the dark entrance of the box behind her and Buckley stalked in. 'Ah, Lord and Lady Croft… and Lady Glenfield, a pleasure!' He bowed slightly.

Lady Croft darted forward and clasped his hands, 'Why have you been sitting on your own this evening William?'

Lady Croft inquired, her voice teasing. 'I tried to beckon you over, but you did not even look up. You just seemed captivated by the stage.'

Buckley took her hand and kissed it, then looked up at her with brooding eyes, 'Lady Croft, I must apologise for my neglect, but tonight I am in a pensive mood and felt a desire to be alone. I do hope you'll excuse my lack of affection.'

Lady Croft kept her hand in his and laughed as she looked round at her companions, 'Well, of course, William, every man has to enjoy a little peace within the hustle and bustle of this world.'

Lord Croft raised both eyebrows, and Buckley met his gaze with a grin. 'Yes, of course, delightful sometimes to be on one's own. But, Lady Croft, I came over on an errand. I would like to extend an invitation to the Race Ball. This year it's being held at the Old Prestbury Manor. Fulwar and his mother Lady Chamberlayne are of course hosting. Lady Glenfield, you will also receive a formal invite.' He nodded at the captivated group.

Lady Croft clapped her hands, 'Oh, we would be delighted to attend!'

Buckley bowed, smiled but then frowned briefly, 'It would be our honour if you could all attend. We are hoping for the support of people such as yourselves with the return of the races nearer to the town.' He paused. 'As you know, there has been...opposition.'

He pronounced the last word slowly. A silence fell within the group.

Lord Croft broke in, 'Oh, Buckley my man, be assured that you have our full support in such matters, along with many other esteemed members of our class. This ridiculous protest against the races is a phase, I can assure you. Of course, we will be at the ball to welcome the return of the races. We wouldn't miss it for the world.'

Buckley nodded sharply and shook Lord Croft's hand

before bowing to the ladies and striding out. Lady Croft and Lady Glenfield stood together in delighted anticipation.

Chapter 5

Fulwar Chamberlayne, the owner of Old Prestbury Manor, stood in its moated grounds overlooking Prestbury Park. His riding boots rested on the edge of a steep bank which swept down into a murky, shallow, spring-fed moat tangled with reeds. Beyond this, a vast expanse of flat land stretched out in front of him.

Fulwar gazed at a moorhen bobbing on the moat for a few moments before lifting his head to look across the park, placing his hand above his eyes to shade them from the sun. His smile widened as he scanned the naturally circular park, his gaze coming to rest on a basic wooden structure. The half-built grandstand was in the distance to the left on the edge of the space, while his old manor, a sprawling building of Cotswold stone, stood on the opposite side of the flat land in a quiet spot with trees hanging over the pond-like moat.

Lord Chamberlayne was known as a Cheltenham eccentric; tall in stature and flamboyant in dress, he was a descendent of the aristocratic Chamberlayne family who had owned the Old Manor and the land surrounding it since the reign of Elizabeth I. Its three hundred acres of land was rented by various leaseholders including Prestbury Park Farm: which consisted of several farm buildings, with a yard, gardens, orchards, and ponds. The manor was served by a small lane near a spring and to the east was the ancient Prestbury Village.

Fulwar swept his dark curly hair off his face as he reached

down for a stick at the side of the moat. He wore red breeches and a large white shirt which billowed out over an ample stomach. He threw the stick over the water and as it landed, he jumped as he felt a slap on the back.

Fulwar whirled around. William Buckley stood behind him, grinning. 'Surveying the turf old man?' Buckley asked.

Fulwar gave a cry of delight and grabbed Buckley by both shoulders. 'Old boy!' Laughing, he spun around again and swept his hand across the panorama of Prestbury Park.

'Yes, I certainly am. Superior form, old boy. Look at it.' Fulwar's easy smile broadened again across his weathered face: a face which was used to the outdoor pursuits of hunting and racing but also to the easy enjoyment of a titled life. Both men now gazed across the park.

Buckley turned to Fulwar, 'It certainly is a sight to behold.' There was a satisfied pause as Buckley took in a deep breath. 'Nothing will stop us this time Fulwar, I for one am making sure of it.'

Fulwar glanced quickly at him before turning back to view the park. 'Of course old boy, the sport will be equal to the races of any former year; if not better. I can assure you that the committee is taking every possible precaution to prevent a repeat of those disgraceful scenes a few seasons ago. They very nearly annihilated the races altogether.' He sighed.

Buckley nodded and frowned, 'Yes, yes, we thankfully found the Andoversford site. But have you heard of the latest sermon from that damned reverend?'

Fulwar wheeled to face Buckley once more. 'Oh, for goodness' sake, no! What is he rallying his flock to do now? I have a good mind to...'

'Don't you worry old chap; it is all in hand this time.' Buckley interrupted and put his hand on his friend's shoulder. There was a pause. Fulwar reached down for another stick as Buckley persisted, 'But, what concerns me is how some of those joining the reverend's ranks are old allies of ours. Magistrate Robinson for one. The letters in the *Cheltenham Chronicle* have erupted once again. It is all anyone talks about at The Club. At least the man's radical followers no longer reside in the town, or so I am told. I have my spies everywhere.' Buckley kicked a stone and it plopped into the moat.

Fulwar's eyes widened, 'Oh, I don't think the puritans will ever take over for good, and you know I don't read the press. No time for it old chap. But do tell me the gist of it.'

Buckley frowned, 'I have no time for it either old man, but after all the strife we have had over the years, I have to keep my eye on it as I am determined these races go ahead. Not only that they go ahead, but I plan to see to it personally that this is the last time the reverend pokes his nose into our business.' He picked up another stone and hurled it into the distance.

Fulwar turned to his friend, 'Come now Buckley, let's leave him to his ways. He'll never stop us completely.'

Buckley stared into the distance, 'He shamed me old man, and everything I stand for.'

Fulwar watched his friend, who quickly looked back at him and smiled broadly. 'Anyway, the gist of it, as always my dear Fulwar, is that the reverend claims he's saving us from eternal destruction. He's been telling his congregation, and of course writing in his little pamphlets that the weeks before the races aren't profitable for the town.'

'Not profitable for the town!' Fulwar roared in disbelief. 'The arrivals during race month undoubtedly increase in rank, fashion, and beauty. My! Just experience any Race Ball and you will know that to be the truth. I anticipate this year's celebration will be especially grand! Did anyone put him in his place?'

'Yes, the editor in fact. As he has done before, he wrote of the long list of names with which so many of the horses appointed to run for our great Gloucestershire Stakes are associated. He challenged Cole to explain how such individuals have been tainted with the guilt of the Racecourse.'

'Quite right, the audacity of the man! Does he not know the importance of some of our patrons even?' Fulwar paused. 'So, what is the pest's point; what is he trying to do?'

'Oh, Chamberlayne my friend, his point is to accuse us; the people who have made Cheltenham as it is today, of attracting the most worthless members of society to the race ground and corrupting the honest poor for the sole purpose of vice. He calls it an ancient festival of the Heathens - that the racecourse is made a perpetual scene of intoxication and debauchery! That's his point and he seems to be increasing his hold over Cheltenham society by the year.' Buckley's voice had now risen to an almost manic laugh.

Fulwar laughed heartily to break the tension. 'Well, what else did the Heathens get up to? I would rather hear more about that than listen to another word of what this straight rod of a preacher is trying to teach me. The likes of you and me Buckley, will never change and as for the honest rustics… if my memory serves me right, I can still picture the groups of fair and innocent labourers up on Cleeve Hill.' He looked up to the hill in the distance and moved his hand across the top. 'To what extent has their virtue been violated by the excursion of the races for a few days of the working year? A few hours of cheap revelry in which they can indulge is good for them. Is he suggesting anything could replace them?'

Buckley looked into the distance again and sighed. 'Let us change the subject. How are our plans progressing here?'

'Well, shall we walk over and have a look old boy?' Fulwar led as he stepped over a wooden bridge crossing the moat at a slight slope. The vast park lay out in front of them and a flock of swallows swooped overhead as they walked across the left side of the circular space towards the grandstand.

'Things are complex my old chap, but all in our favour.' Fulwar sighed, 'If you had been attending committee meetings my dear Buckley, you would be informed. Yes, this damned lease we signed back in 1823, but we can now have the use of three fields for one week a year in July. We are up against it to get our grandstand built.'

'I see.' Buckley raised his eyebrows and nodded. 'And do you think this is the start of something more permanent? We all know the ground was better up at Cleeve.'

'Well yes, but let us get though this year first old boy. Of course, I believe this is our chance to bring the races nearer to the town and make them easier for people to get to. Instead of trudging up that damned hill in the middle of summer, more will be tempted to just walk from the town. It's going to be an even bigger event and it will only infuriate the reverend more.' Fulwar laughed.

Buckley paused before nodding slowly, 'I don't mean to just infuriate him. I mean to stop him.'

The friends had walked across the perimeter of the park. As they reached the grandstand, they came to a pause and looked up. The two-tiered rectangular wooden building had begun to look like the previous structure on Cleeve Hill but without its black and white paint and emblem. It had two staircases on either side leading to a reception room above a stepped balcony. Buckley put his foot on the lower step, looked up at the hill in the distance and sighed. 'Some of my best wins were up at Cleeve you know old boy? I'm wondering what the form will be like here?'

Fulwar tapped his foot on the ground and then jumped up onto the steps, opening his arms out in a celebration of the new site, 'What? Stop thinking about what happened up at Cleeve! Things will be glorious here! Imagine the roar of the racegoers from this stand? It will be heard all over town. Now Buckley, I don't want you to worry about anything. It is all planned out and nothing will go wrong. Our pesky reverend will not get in the way this time.'

Buckley sighed again and smiled, 'And the Race Ball, are plans all in place for next month?'

Fulwar beamed and raised his large eyebrows, 'Yes, mother

has it all in hand. We are delighted to host instead of the usual Assembly Rooms. I'm looking forward to getting up to some mischief, so I hope you've invited lots of your friends so we can jolly well be heathens. It promises to be a lavish affair, and quite a few of the girls I've invited have a kick in their gallop, I can tell you.' He laughed loudly.

Buckley gazed up at the grandstand, 'I am looking forward to it old boy, and to having the races here in Cheltenham again. About time.'

Chapter 6

According to the latest edition of the Looker-On, it had been an uneventful week. However, as Colonel William Buckley strode into the elegant inner room of the Montpellier Spa with his brother Craven, the new MP for Cheltenham, he was finding it anything but. Buckley had uncharacteristically been reading the society pages and discovered it was Maria's place of choice for taking the waters.

Commonly known as Thompson's Spa, subscribers entered from the spacious Grand Promenade to take the waters in the morning and evening. This morning's dispensing was coming to an end, but there were still a few groups of people either drinking or sitting in the main Rotunda pump room. The room was perfectly circular with a high skylight letting in shafts of sunlight which fell on the Roman style columns and leafy plants at the sides of the room.

The arrangements in the Rotunda remained the same as on former seasons, although it had been freshly painted and pictures by the local engraver Mr Gubbin had been rehung. Some old paintings had been removed and several new ones introduced in their place, among which were the portraits of the Reverend Francis Cole, Reverend Wilfred Phillips, and Dr. Willard Thomas – all very good likenesses. The botanical displays were also greatly superior to former seasons and, along with the quantities of beautiful geraniums, cactuses and other hot house plants dispersed about, the company at Montpellier

Spa had the gratification of seeing a very rare specimen: the Night-Blowing Cereus in full bloom and proudly taking centre stage in the Rotunda.

Craven Buckley, taller than his brother but not as well built, had turned to look at the portraits with his narrow eyes in a bid to avoid the stares of the remaining water drinkers, who at first pretended not to notice that two of Cheltenham's most important men had entered the grand room. He knew gentlemen would approach to converse as soon as they considered it polite and, of course, fashionable, without seeming too keen.

Colonel Buckley stood glaring at the likeness of the reverend before sidling up to Craven, 'Annoyed that your portrait isn't adorning the walls yet?' Craven glanced at his older sibling who remained silent. Craven was the first MP for Cheltenham since the Reform Bill which created new constituencies and, like his brother, was known as a bit of a character. Some years ago, Craven had taken up his pistol and fought a duel against the Tory MP for Chippenham, but, mercifully, both men missed their targets. Also like his brother, he had crossed words with the Reverend Cole but on matters of politics, and Craven had accused 'the Pope of Cheltenham' of slander after the reverend had branded him an atheist, infidel, and a scoffer at religion. In more recent times, the MP had endeavoured to shake off this characterful reputation and remained polite and sober at formal gatherings. He stood observing the room.

Buckley sighed, 'Oh Craven, must I really accompany you to these attendances? Anyone would think I'm becoming respectable…and if I have to talk about the next Reform Bill again at any of these sober gatherings, I think I will go quite mad.'

Craven smirked, 'My dear brother, you really didn't need to escort me on my duties. I do not require a chaperone. In fact, I don't know why you're here.' His voice was measured as he nodded to a couple of elderly gentlemen approaching.

Buckley looked about him, 'I'm here in pursuit. A spark

was rekindled at the theatre the other night.' As Craven rolled his eyes at his brother, the object of Buckley's ignited affections glided into the Rotunda. Maria Mount was surrounded by an entourage of brightly dressed ladies and gentlemen of the stage. Their lace trimmed frocks and shirts were a rainbow of colours, competing with the glittering multitude of tiny kaleidoscopes reflecting from the crystal candle holders of the great brass chandelier. The group sauntered to one side of the echoing room, talking and laughing as loudly as if they were performing on stage. Maria wore the brightest dress of the group: an emerald green silk gown which swooped over her voluptuous form. As she stood and commanded the room, all eyes fell upon her. Buckley smiled and bowed as she glanced over. Craven was now in conversation with the two gentlemen who sought answers in the world of politics and parish affairs.

Maria watched, lips pursed, as Buckley swiftly excused himself and approached her with a swagger. He was a full head taller than her and as she looked up at him, he bowed, smiling. 'Miss Mount, a pleasure. I must say, your performance the other night was pure captivation.'

Maria nodded but didn't smile. 'Colonel Buckley, your brother,' she glanced over at Craven whose earnest face contrasted with Buckley's mischievous grin. 'I have seen him here undertaking his duties these past two seasons. I have never seen you here with him, why so?'

Buckley straightened. He enjoyed her playfulness, 'Yes, of course, dear Craven, his admirable duties engross so much of the attention of men, but in truth Miss Mount, as his affairs curdle the milk of human kindness and deaden all our gentler sympathies, I promised I would have nought to do.'

Maria couldn't help but throw her head back in laughter, revealing more of her long, graceful neck as Buckley licked his lips.

Maria's laughter stopped as suddenly as it had begun. 'Then why are you here, William?' she asked, her gaze steady. She looked at him for a long time before turning and walking away to join her group. If he thinks he can twist his way into my life again, she thought. Her blood boiled with both anger and excitement as she tried to focus on her friends' easy chatter.

Unperturbed, Buckley bowed to Maria's departing figure and her lively group before striding over to the marble-tabled water pump. He lifted his hand at the pump attendant and the portly, red-faced woman, who drew the liquid through a beautiful crystal tap, handed him a glass of the Cheltenham waters. Buckley scanned the room, fixing his dark and intense eyes on Maria before tilting the glass and swallowing the murky, sulphurous water in one gulp. Turning to the pump and wincing slightly, he slammed his water glass on the table, turned back again and noticed Maria had moved over to admire the flowering cactus. She talked to an attendant next to the tropical plant.

Buckley watched. He studied the huge tropical plant in more detail. Standing on the table, the plant reached from Maria's hip to above her head. Its climbing stems were wavy and tangled, separated by broad rounded intervals. Small spines and hairs covered the surfaces of the branches which were yellow, brown, and grey in places. But the eye was drawn to the showy white flower in the centre of the plant; a simple trumpet-like blossom which opened to reveal a deep, moist haven of petals.

'It comes from the Americas,' the small man attending the plant explained, smiling at Maria and pointing.

'A more perfect flower was certainly never exhibited…' Maria smiled and gently stroked one of the stems as she bent to smell the specimen.

The attendant nodded enthusiastically, 'It looks like a dead shrub most of the time. But in early summer, the white flower opens to release its delicate fragrance, and the period of blossom lasts for about one week. Its fragrance is difficult to describe but many say it is sweet, or that it reminds them of vanilla.'

Maria bent forward and hovered her nose above the petals. 'Yes, it is a beautiful scent, very unusual. I feel fortunate to have seen such a rare specimen in bloom.' Maria stared at the flower. She thought of the rare moments she spent with her children. Now five and three years old, she wondered if they had flowers to smell; if they enjoyed playing in the garden; if they thought of her as much as she thought of them. Suddenly she felt a confusing and overwhelming urge to either run to Buckley and beg him to marry her so her children could return, or slap him across the face and shout aloud to everyone in the room about what he had put her through over all these years. Maria looked about her, shook her head, and gathered herself.

Buckley continued to stare at Maria as she moved around the room, stopping at the floral displays and talking to admirers. Her easy and smooth voice rose above the general hubbub and Buckley stood watching. As she circled the room, she lighted next to him. Buckley was now in a heightened state and blundered quickly, 'I saw your performance last night. I was captivated.'

Maria sighed, 'You said, Sir. But I thought you meant to change your ways? Can you not resist me again?'

People were now turning to look at the pair. Buckley was gazing down at Maria and gently touched her elbow to guide her to a quieter part of the room. His dark eyes looked intensely into hers, 'I tried to resist... but I cannot. It was for the best Maria. As you know, I am still in the process of laying claim to my inheritance. It is not an easy as you may think. As soon as that is finalised, we shall marry. You have my word.'

Maria lowered her voice, 'Your word, really! Now! I've had many a promise of marriage from you in the past, and it has come to nought. And what of our children?' She looked quickly about her and lowered her voice to a hiss, 'They are to grow up without their real mother because you continue to trick me? They and I have been cast aside by you too many times before.'

Buckley drew closer to Maria. She breathed in his familiar scent of leather and tobacco. For a moment, she closed her eyes.

'Stop it,' she whispered. 'That won't work this time.' Maria pulled away and walked off past the flower specimens but glanced over her shoulder before disappearing through the library and into a small adjoining room. Buckley first glowered and then smiled before looking around and following.

Maria's steps quickened as she headed through the small room to a spiral staircase in the corner. The smell of sulphur strengthened and the rhythmical mechanical sound of the pump room increased as she descended into darkness on the steep steps. Buckley entered the room just as her head bobbed below the opening to the staircase; within two strides he crossed the room, grabbed the ironwork banisters with both hands and plunged into the depths of the cellar behind Maria. As soon as the pair reached the bottom of the stairs, Buckley grabbed his mistress, clasped her firmly round the waist and kissed her in a long, passionate, open-mouthed embrace.

Pushing him away, Maria suddenly slapped him across the cheek. Buckley pulled away, held his cheek briefly as he looked to the floor and then looked up again into her eyes. He put his hands gently on her shoulders. His face showed concern, 'I understand your frustration, Maria.' The light was dim, and the rhythmical clunking of the nearby water pump nearly drowned out his words. Maria moved towards him and shouted into his ear.

'You must give me better than your word William! We must marry now if I am to be with our children. Have you no sense at all of what this means to me? Do you know what I have been through, giving up our children?' Maria suddenly grabbed the silver locket around her neck and opened it. The little portraits were barely visible in the weak light, but Buckley stared at them. There was a fleeting expression in his face which Maria had never witnessed before: a moment of pure tenderness and softness. He gently closed the locket and stroked it as it rested on her chest.

'I promise my love, I promise Maria. Once I have my title, we can all be together.' She sighed deeply as Buckley started to kiss her neck, slowly moving his lips from behind her ear to her collarbone and down to her breast. 'You are irresistible Maria… you do know that? You have my word.' Buckley murmured as he looked up from her bodice with brooding eyes.

'Why do you play with my heart so?' Maria sighed feebly as Buckley kissed her again, then took her by the waist and lifted her up onto a dusty stone ledge. He brushed his hand down her long skirt, lifting the edge, and moved his hand along her white stockinet leg, feeling for the soft skin of her thigh and beyond. Maria arched, throwing her head back as she gasped and moaned, but the sound was drowned out by the rhythmical clunking, sucking, and flushing of the water pump.

Chapter 7

Deanswood Villa stood in two acres of gardens with stables and an outhouse. It had been Maria's Cheltenham home since the property was built four years previously. Her increasing popularity had resulted in a healthy income, and with the help of a number of pacifying payments from Buckley, she had been able to buy it for herself. A sweeping drive led up to the grand three-storey home. On one side of the house was a large croquet lawn, with a summerhouse and the whole scene was surrounded with herbaceous borders. Little paths in a kitchen garden were edged with minute box hedges, not more than nine inches high. While on the other side of the house, the area was wilder, and a large weeping willow stood. A lonely little swing hung from its strong branches while its delicate willowing leaves swept down and stroked the lawn. Shaded unattended plants grew up to tangle into the swing.

Instead of her dear children, Maria's odious parents lived in her Cheltenham home, and having faced bankruptcy, contributed very little to their upkeep. Mr and Mrs Mount believed they were owed a restful life of being provided for, and told many that they were the sole reason behind their daughter's rise to fame, having introduced her to the stage at an early age. Maria felt she had no choice but to house them.

This bright morning, Mr Mount was sat with his wife in the drawing room. A tall narrow man with a long nose and shifting eyes, he wore a long frayed purple cloak with gold brocade around the edges which he wrapped around him in his armchair. Mrs Mount sat opposite. Barely half the height of her husband but twice the width, the lady had the same dimples as her daughter, but her mouth turned down at the edges and the lines on her faced indicated that her most commonly worn expression was a frown. The small, plump lady sank into a cushioned sofa and peered into the *Cheltenham Chronicle.*

'Outstanding reviews for Maria's performance Mr Mount. We should probably go along, don't you think?' She gave a high-pitched laugh.

Mr Mount sniffed, 'Well, perhaps, but I have played many a Romeo in my time, and I've seen her play Juliet before. I say, I don't know what all the fuss about her is! But it doesn't hurt to revisit old roles, as long she gets paid more! It is quite remarkable. Our dear little girl. She certainly didn't have the talent growing up.' He looked down and picked at the gold brocade on his cloak, 'I think it's all down to me you know, my dear. I could have been someone on the stage if it wasn't for bringing up Maria and giving her all our care and attention.'

Mrs Mount nodded, murmured something unintelligible and buried her head in the paper.

At the top of the house Maria stood outside two rooms which only she ever visited. The first was a room for a nanny. It held a small, simple wooden bed which was made up with cream bedclothes. The bed had an empty shelf over its head and pictures adorned the white walls along with a framed piece of embroidery. It had been carefully created by Maria when she was a child. Its red embroidered letters spelled 'Home Sweet Home' around a bright purple flower.

Next to this small room was Maria's favourite room in the house: the nursery. Two small beds were made up neatly side-by-side in the centre of the space. In front of a large window, a round table displayed a number of neatly laid out toys, including a wooden spinning top, a jack in the box, some soldiers, and a porcelain doll with soft brown hair. Two small chairs sat forlornly at the sides of the table. Pride of place along from the window was an immaculate rocking horse. It's red, green, and yellow painted sides were unchipped, and its leather bridle was shiny and unworn. The horse looked proud but almost sad, thought Maria as she stood in the middle of the room and gazed around. A beam of sunlight cast across the floor to reach the horse's tail. Maria walked towards it and stretched out her hand to stroke the chestnut brown hair. She thought of her brown-haired children and wondered what it would be like to stroke their heads and hold their little bodies tight and never let them go. She wiped away a tear and walked out of the room as she heard footsteps coming up the stairs. It was Hetty.

'Madam, I have a note for you.'

Maria rushed to the landing and took the note with a smile, then returned into the nursery and sank down on one of the little chairs. 'Oh, William.' She whispered to herself as she quickly opened the letter and read it.

Maria cried out, and then pressed her hand to her mouth. From the top of the stairs, Hetty came dashing back into the nursery.

'Miss? What is it?' Hetty stood at the door gazing at her mistress. Maria had placed the note on the toy table and was now crying softly.

'Ah, Hetty, it is just a note from Mr Hayne... He is to be delayed for our meeting. It is nothing... I just thought it was from someone else... no matter.' Maria brushed away her tears and her voice broke. Hetty stood still in the middle of the room and folded her arms. Maria looked up at her and sighed.

'Oh Hetty, I thought it was from William.' She laughed nervously. 'Of course, it wouldn't be. When was the last time he sent a note or even visited?'

The maid stood looking at her mistress for a while and then stepped closer. 'Madam, if I may say... I think that Mr

Hayne would be a good match...perhaps he will understand your situation? This situation.' She glanced around the room and bit her lip.

Maria stared at her maid. Hetty had always been loyal, and this was her second year as part of her staff. Over time, she had shown both great tolerance of Mr. Mount and his barked-out orders, and she had been very kind to Maria when she was tired after her performances and when she sensed her mistress's sadness. Hetty knew many intimate matters relating to her mistress, including her continued involvement with Buckley.

'Oh Hetty, I know you know everything, and you're right. I can't stay the way I am, always waiting for that man to marry me. Come and sit dear. You are so young, and I hope you make the right choices in life. Not like me. I cannot talk to mother or father about any of this.'

Hetty smiled, tentatively walked over and then sat in the opposite little chair. The sight of her in the tiny child's chair made her mistress smile. 'Madam, I am young, but I feel I know you well and understand what you want in life, but...'

'Let me tell you a bit about my life, Hetty, and you'll wonder why I put up with those two downstairs. And perhaps you'll even understand more than that.' Maria paused and looked out of the window as she wondered where to begin.

Maria took a deep breath, 'Father is much older than mother... 25 years older. Her family had a fortune when he married her, but he was only a theatre manager. Mother was a great beauty but very innocent and, once she met my father; her parents withdrew all support or interest. They eloped and returned to Plymouth, but gradually my father squandered all the little money Mother brought with her and gave her little attention. I came along and was ushered into their world. My father's whole life was the theatre. Mother would withdraw, but I became bound up in it and was allowed to watch plays from a very early age.' Maria paused as she recalled her childhood, and Hetty gave her a reassuring smile.

'We had very few friends and by the age of twelve, I was acting on the Plymouth stage. I grew up in this world: it's all I've ever known. I wanted to be an actress. I didn't see anything wrong with it. Now I know it's not the life any decent father and mother would desire for their daughter if they wanted to keep her safe.' Maria wiped away a tear.

Hetty sat and listened, wide-eyed.

Maria shook her head and carried on. 'Then, I came to Cheltenham, in the summer of 1826.' Maria stared out of the window briefly before turning back to the maid. She picked up a spinning top and began to twist it on the table. 'I was engaged to perform at the Cambray Theatre in the starring role. Colonel Buckley was there to watch on the first night, but there was hardly anyone else there. He came into my dressing room and started to brag about being an amateur of the stage. He even recited a few lines from a play. He offered to perform with me and ensured a house packed to the rafters. Well, he was as good as his word, and the performances were quite a sensation. People came from far and wide to see him in the play. Of course, he isn't as good as he thinks he is, but... we had a lot of fun. There were parties at his home, and we gradually became close. He told me of his situation... his claim to a title early on. But his obsession with me... he declared his love for me... I didn't think.' Maria laughed at the memory. 'He used to make me laugh, he would say that no one could accuse him of having extraordinary acting talent, but the audience always seemed amused to see him on stage. There was a time when he bombarded me with notes. He would turn up at my door and in my changing room...' Maria's words tailed off; her voice was quiet.

Hetty sighed. 'But what about when you were in childbed Miss... where was he then?'

Maria paused. 'I...I just thought he was going to marry me; I was convinced because of all his promises. I felt excited. But then... then... I was sent away Hetty. This is how these things are done. My father told everyone I was ill. He was very matter-of-fact about it all. We concealed the births as I retreated to the country for my confinement. The children then remained with wet-nurses and foster families. They have been with their current family for two years now.'

Hetty sighed again, 'I did not know all this Miss. I did not know about Mr and Mrs Mount. I knew of Buckley of course, everyone in Cheltenham does I'm afraid Miss. If I had been your maid earlier, I could have warned you. I think you must look to the future. Perhaps Mr Hayne… he is a man of means.' Made confident by Maria's show of trust, Hetty ventured, 'Perhaps your dear children could come and live with us Miss. Tell me, what are they like?'

Maria smiled. It was a smile that lit up her face. 'Oh, they are simply adorable. Jane is the eldest, she's five now and has the sweetest little dimples. I'm told she loves to dance, just like me when I was her age. Jack is three and a little mischief maker, but always happy.' Maria took off her locket and opened it, placing it in front of Hetty.

'The Harrison's, the family who are caring for them, they write to me every three months or so. I keep the letters in here.' Maria jumped up from the chair, moved to a chest at the side of the room and opened one of the top drawers. She carefully brought out a rectangular wooden box and placed it in front of Hetty on the table.

'Open it.' Maria gestured to the box.

Hetty lifted an unlocked brass catch and opened the lid. Inside was a stack of letters carefully tied with blue ribbon. The maid looked up at her mistress and smiled.

'Oh Miss, I didn't know you had all these. I bet you read them all the time?'

Maria nodded. Her smile dropped suddenly as she sighed, and brushing away a tear looked away towards the door, took a deep breath and rose from her chair. She looked down at the little doll. She picked it up in her trembling hand. It was pristine: its blue cotton dress was neat and pressed and the doll itself was unworn and spotless.

Hetty lowered her voice, 'Do you think you will ever get them back Miss?'

'I don't know Hetty, but it's all I ever think of. Tucking them up here in their beds and reading a story.' Maria looked mournfully over at the two beds. She was close to tears again.

Hetty closed the box of letters and put her hand on her mistress's arm. 'Madam, would you read me the note from Mr Hayne?'

Maria stroked the doll's hair, put it carefully back on the table and picked up the note from her admirer.

Chapter 8

As dusk descended onto the newly landscaped Pittville Lake, the sky turned an unusually bright orange before changing to pink and finally to a dusty grey. The Pittville Spa had been completed and opened four years previously at an immense expense to the owner Joseph Pitt and had enjoyed an initial flurry of favouritism in Cheltenham.

The building was situated on rising ground and the architecture both within and without was on a grand scale, with a colonnade encircling the lower part of the pump room and a much-ornamented dome completing the whole. A broad gravel walk from the centre of the building conducted visitors down to a pretty lake at each end of which was an ornamental stone bridge. Beyond the water were two pleasure gardens and an abundance of walks which promised very agreeable shade when the trees attained their full size.

Joseph Hayne stood at the edge of the lake at the foot of the broad gravel walk. He wore a spotless coat, as if it had just been made. He had joined numerous other spectators being amused by a dozen or so miniature ships which sailed and tacked amongst the swans and ducks.

The group of Cheltenham's well-to-do, along with newcomers and visitors like himself, had been personally invited to attend a public meeting at the Pittville Pump Rooms to hear of Mr Pitt's plans for development. Joseph surveyed the crowd and then turned to his solicitor Mr Bebb; a tall and wiry man who rarely smiled and preferred to listen rather than talk. The pair followed the now moving crowd up the gravel path towards the pump rooms, which were lit by a string of gas lights from end to end. The huge columned building of Cotswold stone loomed in front of them; its small green domed roof with three grand standing statues above the colonnade's pillars were backlit by a full moon.

Joseph walked by his solicitor's side and spoke quickly and loudly, 'We know Mr Pitt is doing well. I hear the rooms cut up the other spa proprietors for a time.' He turned to his solicitor who kept his eyes resolutely front. 'Being the new thing of course, I have been told frequently that it was quite unfashionable to think of drinking any other than the Pittville Waters and I have seen engravings of it in several shop windows in Montpellier and on the high street.'

Mr Bebb paused a while before answering, 'There was promise and it became quite the favourite for a short while. But Mr Hayne,' he now turned to his young client, 'Pittville Spa is at the distance of a mile from the centre of the town. It certainly is a magnificent pump room, and it has certainly cost Mr Pitt a great deal, but four years have now elapsed since it opened and I think most company still frequent Thompson's pump room, if I'm not mistaken.' Mr Bebb paused again. The pair were now halfway up the gravel path. 'I have heard Mr Pitt plans to compete with the proposals for zoological gardens within The Park in the south of the town. Perhaps he intends to discuss his plans and appeal for funds, for I have heard this is his way...' Mr Bebb's words tailed off.

Joseph's loud voice caused a few to turn and look at him, 'Well, I think it is a jolly good idea my man. It is all the rage in London and I for one can only see a zoological garden being a success in Cheltenham. I would like to be part of it, if that is what the gentleman is asking for: shareholders?' He turned and smiled at those nearby.

Mr Bebb simply nodded once as they walked up the stone

steps and through a pair of huge stone entrance columns. Joseph paused to look back down the sweeping drive: he made out a few silhouettes of Cheltenham's buildings and the spire of St Mary's Church in the distance.

Inside the pump rooms, Joseph gasped. The building was unlike any other spa. A vast ballroom extended into a rectangular shape. A raised platform was situated at one end, with seating set up facing towards it in preparation for the forthcoming talk, but for a moment all Joseph could think about was dancing with Miss Mount in the opulent space. Her dress whirling and her cheeks flushed as they danced in formation with other couples.

A high ceiling opened out in the centre to a first-floor balcony, then a second, and finally to a ceiling dome to rival that of Montpellier Spa. The dome was smaller but no less impressive due to its height and had surround patterns of decorative roses painted gold and white. A grand chandelier extended from the centre of the dome and its gas lit crystal candle holders sparkled and cast glittering lights across the room.

Joseph and his solicitor walked across the ballroom, nodding to the many other invitees, and then over to the water pump. It was enclosed in a tall wooden and marble statue-like plinth with engravings on the side and topped with a flamboyant stone leaf embellishment. Two large iron handles lay at the sides of the pump with a ledge for glasses and other vessels for the morning and evening pumping.

'Quite revolting!' a lady was explaining the taste of the waters at a laughing companion. 'But the more disgusting, the better the cure they say.' At that moment, there was the sound of a bell and a man announced for everyone to be seated. Joseph and Mr Bebb were among the first to respond and took their places near to the raised platform. Mr Bebb kept his face forward while Joseph turned to smile and grin at those sitting around him.

There was polite chatter, but soon the seats were full, and a hush descended the room as Mr Pitt walked onto the stage. He was an average sized man with a pleasant, friendly face, gentle blue eyes, and a small mouth; he was balding but retained white tufts of hair over his ears. He was wearing a smart brown coat with gold buttons, and a white necktie modest about his neck. He stood on the platform and waited for quiet before he opened his arms and spoke in a smooth and measured voice. 'Welcome friends to this evening's gathering.' Mr Pitt smiled and looked out across the audience.

'As you know, my glorious pump room has now been open for four successful years. Our waters are the best in Cheltenham and have been recommended by a number of eminent doctors in the town.'

Mr Bebb leaned over to Joseph and whispered, 'Shareholders, Sir.'

Joseph stared straight ahead at Mr Pitt who continued, 'Our anniversary breakfasts are well attended with visitor numbers increasing modestly. But, friends, I am here to speak to you this evening not of past successes, but of future endeavours. You may have heard of other developments in Montpellier and Lansdown or in the south of the town at The Park, or perhaps you have even been invited to contribute further private capital to provide elegant public buildings, gracious tree-lined avenues, and prestigious amenities such as parks and gardens to attract more wealthy visitors to Cheltenham.' He paused, surveying the room. 'Well, I have invited you as very important guests today to hear first of my plans to establish a zoological garden right here in Pittville to rival, and with your investment, surpass any of those other developments within the town.'

There was a murmuring in the audience.

Mr Pitt smiled and reached his arms out, 'Firstly, Pittville gains ground in public estimation every year, and its rising plantations, gardens, walks and promenades become every day more beautiful.'

Joseph nodded to his solicitor and those around him.

Mr Pitt continued, 'Rising numbers attend our annual fetes and the number of new and elegant villas along the approaches are still rising. This is confirmation of the strong and increasing influence which our establishment exercises over public opinion and the destinies of the north of the town.'

Mr Pitt paused again and opened his palm towards the map of his Pittville Estates on a wall display behind him. An ambitious web of walks, crescents, parks and gardens could be clearly seen. He smiled again at the audience and continued, 'Now my friends, you may have heard how in London in Regent's Park, a new zoological garden has been established. Used for the purpose of scientific study, there are now plans to open it to the public and we have been told that the latest collection includes the Tower of London menagerie, which boasts a tiger, leopards, a hyena, a large baboon, and various types of monkeys, wolves, and birds. We would aim to replicate London's success, and despite reports of several other zoological gardens being planned across the country, I am confident that we would surpass them all here in Cheltenham! I would like to invite you to consider my exciting plans and what your investment could return.'

Mr Pitt's voice had now become more animated, and his eyes danced across the audience. Gasps and exclamations of 'Wonderful!' 'Imagine!' and 'Well I never!' could be heard throughout the room and there was an eruption of talk while Mr Pitt stood back and smiled. Joseph turned to his solicitor, 'My goodness, imagine it man!'

Mr Bebb blinked quickly and simply nodded.

Joseph nudged him, 'Come on Bebb, this is something I can really get my teeth into. It really is quite a superb idea, isn't it?' Joseph looked searchingly at his solicitor, and finding little to replicate his enthusiasm, turned back round to face the audience which was still in a heightened state of excitement. Joseph grinned.

'Now,' Mr Pitt put up his hand to speak. He laughed as stewards hushed the audience.

'Now, now, my friends, to practical matters. I plan to acquire from Mr Hale Jessop's nursery garden near St James' Square a racoon and some American grey squirrels. I then plan to establish the Cheltenham Zoological Society with some close business associates, and we are confident that this will be both attractive to the public and commercially profitable. It is proposed that the initial outlay of the project can be funded by the sale of one thousand shares at ten pounds each. We also have the support of the London Regent's Park Zoological Gardens, and the committee we formed to find an eligible site has selected a parcel of land just north of the pump rooms.'

The audience erupted once again, and Mr Pitt's talk ended with clear instructions as to how to invest in the project and the proposed returns: estimated income and profit. By this point Joseph was shifting in his seat with excitement and was determined to be the first to speak to the celebrated developer. As soon as Pitt walked off the platform towards the audience, the young investor bounded towards him and was the first to shake his hand.

'Ah, Mr Hayne, From Staffordshire I believe?' Mr Pitt's eyes sparkled.

'You have done your research I see.' Joseph stood wide-eyed and then bowed slightly while his solicitor stood mute beside him.

'We were quite selective with our invitees.' At this remark, Mr Bebb glanced around the packed room and at those waiting behind them. He raised an eyebrow. Joseph beamed with pride and puffed up his chest.

'Well, Mr Pitt. I am certainly impressed with your pump rooms. Quite the talk in my London club, and I imagine the talk of Cheltenham too. I must say immediately that I for one would be delighted to invest in your ambitious project.' Joseph leaned towards the developer.

Mr Bebb stared intently at Mr Pitt as he smiled at Joseph and then shook the young man's hand again.

'We would be delighted to have you as an investor and I can guarantee the success of the project,' Mr. Pitt exclaimed. 'We are getting the paperwork ready for keen supporters to invest this very evening.' Mr Pitt nodded at Mr Bebb who crossed his arms. The developer then turned back to Joseph, to whom he had immediately warmed. 'But tell me, what of your other plans, Mr Hayne? Are you planning to settle here in Cheltenham?'

Joseph nodded and lent in even nearer to Pitt, 'Between you and me Mr Pitt, yes, I am keen to settle in Cheltenham, and...' he blushed slightly. 'I am determined to find a wife. I may be a young fellow, but I am ready to settle down and this might as well be the place. I admire men like you who have capitalised on the booming business. I for one cannot see it abating any time soon. I can see myself and my investments doing well here.' Joseph looked at his elder earnestly.

'I can assure you it is still a booming business,' Pitt's eyes shifted across the room for a moment and then he laughed. 'Ah, and even when it comes to marriage, you will not be short of potential suitors here in Cheltenham my friend. But be careful; there are quite a few ladies ready to seduce those with fortune with their flirtatious words and glances.' He laughed again and patted Joseph on the arm.

Joseph frowned slightly, 'Ah, well, I have no interest in fortune hunters or social climbers; I am looking for a love match.'

Mr Pitt smiled and nodded, briefly turning to Mr Bebb who grimaced in reply before the Pittville developer expressed his extreme gratitude for Joseph's investment and moved on to the line of people waiting to make his acquaintance.

Chapter 9

It was a fine early June morning as Elizabeth Cole walked out of Lansdown House with her daughter Isobel and her housemaid Sarah and led them along the curve of Lansdown Crescent towards Montpellier. Elizabeth had left the reverend at home teaching their son tracts from the Bible.

Despite being small and quiet, Elizabeth held a gentle persuasion over the reverend. She had adored him for many years before their marriage, and he had admired her commitment to the church and his mission in Cheltenham. Elizabeth had long been a member of his devoted flock who believed in his desire to create a number of free schools in the town to enable the spread of education and healthy morals. Theirs was a partnership of both love and mutual respect over this most earnest of issues, but Elizabeth had managed to inject some pleasures into their lives, especially when the children came along. They would often go on family carriage rides into the hills around the town and Elizabeth had introduced the idea of taking cake and lemonade with them. At first, the reverend frowned on some of her ideas, but soon realised the value of the simple and honest pleasures to be shared with his wife and children.

This morning, Elizabeth was pleased with herself for persuading her husband to allow her a visit to the new Montpellier shops. The reverend's annual 'Buns and Tea' event was rapidly approaching. Her husband and a number of the town's clergy did their utmost to dissuade people from going to the races by giving all the school children who avoided the festival free buns and tea on the Well Walk. Tracts were distributed and sermons preached everywhere. In the previous year, 760 children from the different National and Sunday church schools sat down to tea along with the clergy at the tables arranged along the Well Walk. The area was usually given a wide berth by racegoers who congregated on the high street.

'Would it be a good idea to ask those new proprietors of the Montpellier shops to contribute to your charitable cause, my dear?' Elizabeth had asked her husband the previous evening.

'I had not thought of it.' The reverend answered after a long pause. 'But I trust your judgement Elizabeth, and if it only encourages some of these people to be part of everything which is moral and upright in this society, instead of feeding the sensual desires of its ungodly inhabitants and visitors, then I am to be grateful.'

Elizabeth nodded and let her husband have the final word before smiling at Sarah and retiring to bed.

Now, as Elizabeth walked hand-in-hand with Sarah and her young daughter past the squat oval-shaped Mawe and Tatlow Museum and onto the grand Montpellier Pump Room, she felt a surge of excitement. They had never visited the new shops before. Elizabeth was usually at home with the children or attending one of her husband's many sermons or charitable missions, and now she wanted to relish every moment of freedom. Because her intentions were good, she felt no guilt at all in her venture.

They passed Mr Brown's Coffee and Cigar Divan at the corner of the promenade: a favoured resort she knew was exclusively for gentlemen to enjoy a cigar and a cup of coffee. The door was open, and Elizabeth stopped to catch a glimpse of the grandeur inside: a large room resembled a far eastern tent with rich red drapery festooned around the high windows and walls decorated with the glories of fable. Amidst this luxurious oriental décor, dark wood oblong tables stretched along the middle of the room while men lounged around the edges on padded seats sipping, smoking, reading, and conversing. Smoke lingered in the air above the room and around the door, and the sweet scent drifted outside onto the walk. Her daughter stood wide eyed and quiet beside her. Sarah giggled.

Elizabeth did not linger as she knew where she was headed. She looked down the walk and, in the distance, she spotted the large sign of The Jar and Pineapple. She stood and stared in determination at the giant gold pineapple and then walked closer to the door of the shop. Elizabeth encountered the view of its large windows with jars packed with sweets and the delightful smell simultaneously: the light scent of roses combined with a deeper scent of honeyed sweetness.

Opening the door to this delightful emporium, Elizabeth at once felt overwhelmed and the small party stood for a moment on the threshold, drinking it all in. As it was early in the morning, with most of society still in the pump room, the shop was empty: its delicate tables were neatly set with white tablecloths and vases of sweet peas. Steam emanated from the back room and faint hissing and tinkling sounds drifted out. Elizabeth looked around at the pale orange walls and stared at a large painting: a narrow street scene depicting what she imagined was somewhere abroad. The shop was so removed from daily life, she felt as if in a dream.

A loud cough startled her from her daze, and Elizabeth turned her head quickly to see a man standing behind the counter.

'Mr Bonfils?' Elizabeth approached the copper counter and matched the wide smile of the man standing behind it. Her daughter and maid stood behind, still looking wide-eyed around the room.

'Yes *mesdames*, it is I. What is your pleasure on this fine morning?' The Frenchman smiled kindly at the group, smoothed down his white apron and then pulled a bowl of pastel coloured icing-sugar drops from the side of the counter to rest between them. 'Please try my latest creation. It is something I have been experimenting with.'

Elizabeth felt at once at ease as she glanced down at the sweets and then looked back up at the confectioner. She was so unused to eating treats, she shook her head, 'Oh, well, no Sir, it is far too early for such, a…'

The confectioner waved his arm as if swiping away any doubt, 'Oh *madame*, please! There is no one else here to try them.' He beckoned the little girl and maid to come forward and cupped the small bowl in both hands. 'Now, these have been made from the finest of ingredients, including petals picked by my own hands from the *Jardin des Plantes* in Paris. You must try!'

'Oh Mother, please can we try?' Isobel grasped Elizabeth's hand and looked up at her wide-eyed.

Elizabeth looked behind her at the door then bowed her head towards the bowl before briefly looking up at Mr Bonfils and smiling her permission. She picked up a pink drop, the pretty handcrafted circle beautiful against her cream glove, then took up another two and handed one to Isobel, and one to Sarah. She placed the sweet carefully into her mouth. Elizabeth closed her eyes to savour the exotic sweetness of the drop, but quickly opened them again and looked at her daughter whose eyes were wide. The little girl made a murmuring sound and smiled up at her mother. Their host rested his elbows on the counter, his hands under his chin.

'I do enjoy watching people taste my creations,' he laughed quietly and brought another dish before his new customers, but Elizabeth put her hand to her mouth and shook her head as she finished the sweet and smiled.

'Please Mr Bonfils, it is such a delight and I have truly never tasted anything like this before. But my mission here today is not in pursuit of my own pleasure.' She paused. 'My husband, the Reverend Cole, you have heard of him?'

Mr Bonfils nodded slowly, 'Yes, the reverend, although I am new here, I have heard of him.'

Elizabeth saw that no explanation of her husband's influence was needed. 'If I may be so forward, I wanted to ask if you would contribute to an event which benefits the hundreds of children who attend our free schools here in Cheltenham. Not only has my husband founded schools here but three years ago he also opened the first free church in the town, where the poor might be accommodated as well as the rich. It is thanks to the generosity of Cheltenham citizens who have joined my husband's cause that we are able to host a Buns and Tea party on the Well Walk on the day of the Races. If you would be able to offer anything to the event, we would be most grateful for your contribution.'

The confectioner put a finger to his lips, squinted his eyes, nodded at the request and then disappeared wordlessly into the back room. Elizabeth stood in wonder listening to the rummaging of pots and pans until Mr Bonfils reappeared holding an oblong shaped container aloft. The white porcelain mould had impressions of berries and leaves and fluted sides.

'Now, I will make my lemon jelly from my very own secret recipe!' he proudly announced with a sweep of his arm. The little girl and maid giggled. 'I make it in a special way, and I garnish with pieces of fruit and whipped cream for decoration.' Mr Bonfils waved his hands flamboyantly as he described his creation to be.

Elizabeth beamed, 'Well, that is very generous of you! I am sure my husband will be most grateful. May we invite you to our home as a gesture of thanks?'

'Oh no, it is my pleasure really, but I would like to come and see their little faces as they taste my delight at the Teas and Buns event, if I may? Myself and my staff will be honoured to deliver the jellies personally.'

Elizabeth nodded and laughed, 'Yes, of course, we would love to see you on the day.' She paused, 'You are not a racegoer Mr Bonfils?'

The confectioner shook his head, 'No, no, I prefer working

in my shop, as I am dedicated to my customers, and I am sure the walks will be busy at certain times with those visitors to the races. And I believe gamblers are gentlemen who have nothing more meaningful to do with their lives...' He raised his eyebrows. 'But here, taste these, please.' While he was talking, Mr Bonfils had placed another glass bowl before his customer.

Elizabeth glanced down and laughed. The glossy sweets were a creamy light brown colour. She picked three up and handed them to her daughter and maid again before opening her mouth and placing a sweet on her tongue. Just as Elizabeth closed her eyes to savour the moment, the door of the shop swung open. Two ladies walked in as Elizabeth watched.

The elder of the two women was finely dressed and had dark hair and striking, wide brown eyes. The younger of the two, Elizabeth noticed, looked at Sarah and gave a small nod. She must be a maid too, Elizabeth thought.

'Madame Mount! What a pleasure to see you here again!' Mr Bonfils' low bow suggested to Elizabeth that this was a lady of great importance. She stared at the ladies, unable to wrench her gaze from the beautiful woman.

'Miss Mount, let me introduce you to Madame Cole, the wife of our good town Reverend. Madame Cole, Miss Mount who is appearing at The Cambray Theatre this season.' Mr Bonfils moved to the side and opened his arms in a wide gesture of welcome to all within his shop.

Elizabeth nodded kindly at Maria and blushed slightly, 'Oh, a pleasure.'

For a moment Maria was quiet. Her eyes lingered on Isobel as she took in her brown curls and smiling upturned face. She was still sucking her sweet and her wide eyes were full of wonder at both the taste of the caramel and the arrival of such a glamorous lady. The actress felt a pang of pain in her stomach and suddenly, stepped towards the girl and exclaimed, 'Oh, how you look like... how I wish I could bring my daughter here!'

Both maids gasped, but then there was a pause and Elizabeth slowly nodded her head and smiled kindly at Maria.

'Miss Mount, such a pleasure to meet you. My daughter has certainly enjoyed her first visit.' She smiled lovingly at Isobel who, embarrassed by all the attention, moved to hold her mother's side. 'But if you will excuse us.' Elizabeth turned to the confectioner who awkwardly stood in the middle of them with his arms wide. 'Please Mr Bonfils; I must be on my way. Thank you so much for your generous offer and we will look forward to your delivery on the morning of the event.'

Maria shook her head slightly, her fingers clasped briefly around her silver locket, before smiling at Elizabeth and moving closer to the counter. Elizabeth held her daughter's hand, looked back, nodded, and smiled once more to the actress before walking out onto the Grand Promenade.

Maria sat on a chair near the counter, shook her head again and laughed. 'Well, I am surprised to see the reverend's wife visiting the new shops, especially yours Mr Bonfils!' The confectioner had now returned behind the counter. 'But I can imagine it would be hard for most to keep away from the pleasures on offer here.' She clapped her hands, looked at Hetty and then back to Mr Bonfils. 'Now, I have come early to escape the rush and to try your wonderful ice cream!'

Mr Bonfils bowed and sprang into action. He clicked his fingers, shouted 'Ice!' and a young boy rushed out from the back room with a shallow wooden crate and a short, blunt knife. He was out of the door in seconds and sprinting across the walk and into the Montpellier Gardens.

'I must say, you do have an efficient service here Mr Bonfils.' Maria laughed. 'I find it amazing that you can collect the ice from deep inside a cave in the gardens and within minutes you create a freezing masterpiece!'

The confectioner simply smiled as he took a copper pan from the wall and disappeared into the back room.

'I will probably be calling by again very soon Mr Bonfils.'

Maria called after him. 'A certain Mr Hayne has asked me to escort him on a turn of the gardens and I will no doubt bring him here.' She sighed to herself. Buckley had not been in contact with her since their meeting at the pump rooms. She berated herself that once again he had used her for his own pleasure. It seemed she only ever held brief power over him when he wanted one thing from her. Oh, to be a reverend's wife, she thought. Surely, a simpler existence.

In no time at all, the young boy with the crate returned. The vessel held a heap of coarse sided, thick white glossy blocks of various sizes. Maria saw crystals sparkling in the bottom of the crate as it was whisked past her and into the sugar foundry beyond. She heard a bang and then the crushing, shaking, and scraping of the freezing mixture, and a further tinkling of pots accompanied by the joyful singing of Mr Bonfils. Then, within minutes, the confectioner appeared from behind the counter with his ice cream creation: a perfectly round pink ice bombe within a delicate glass bowl. The sphere of frosted ice had the impression of little roses all around it and was topped with a pale pink rose petal.

'Oh, how divine!' Maria clapped her hands together before picking up the dainty spoon Mr Bonfils had placed beside the bowl. Scooping up a small amount, Maria tasted the ice and her eyes closed with pleasure and delight. She laughed, 'I have never tasted anything like it! Oh Hetty, you must try.' Maria requested another spoon and the maid helped herself. Her eyes widened at the luxury of the taste.

Mr Bonfils stood behind the counter, smoothed down his apron, and smiled.

Chapter 10

The showers which had fallen on the mid-June morning had given fresh life and beauty to every leaf and flower along the walks and gardens, and the air was loaded with a perfume that might almost be felt. Many visitors to Montpellier now preferred the Promenade to the Pump Room and chose to listen to the band under the free vault of heaven rather than beneath the dome of the Rotunda.

The Jar and Pineapple had become one of the most popular shops on the Grand Promenade. There were daily queues outside the shop and a custom had grown up for ices to be eaten in the gardens opposite, or even in carriages under the trees. Ladies would remain in their equipages, their escorts leaning against the railings near them, while the white-coated waiters dodged across the road with their orders straight out of the moulds before they began to melt, and then sped away again.

This morning, Hetty hovered near Maria Mount and Joseph Hayne as they promenaded along the main walk of the Montpellier Gardens. It was the actresses' second meeting with the young man. The first had been a promenade of the Well Walk. The pair had talked about the London theatres under the towering elm trees and arranged to meet again at The Jar and Pineapple. Maria had introduced her new admirer to the delights of Mr Bonfils' ices, and they had sat on an ornamental bench next to the Montpellier Gardens each enjoying a peach ice. Joseph had been as excited as Maria about the new shop. In his exuberance, she had found a renewed enjoyment of Cheltenham; she felt lighter and almost carefree as she showed off the town's pleasures to the newcomer.

Now, as they walked along the neat shrub-lined paths, Joseph pointed to the brightly painted red and green Chinese pagoda where the band performed a Waterloo battle march with vigour. He tapped his hand against his breeches and then did a mock soldier's march across the front of the newly painted pagoda coming to rest at a marble fountain. Maria was charmed by his playfulness and smiled at her companion. Now standing in front of the marble fountain sculpted with a cherub holding a swan, the pair watched a number of water jets springing from the rockwork around the edge of the large basin and up into the marble one above. The water glistened with gold and silver fish which darted around and through the water jets.

'Such a pretty effect.' said Joseph. 'I hear the jets of water are operated by a steam engine sited in the Montpellier Laboratory, and I was told that when in full force, they can be thrown 32 ft into the air.' Joseph quickly raised his right arm to signal the jet, a motion which made his companion jump and then laugh.

'Quite remarkable,' Maria's eyes widened. 'I do know it has quite a story. It is Italian but became the property of the French during the war and after passing through several hands, it was sold to Thomas Henney, the proprietor of the Sherborne Spa.' The actress turned to face the direction of the spa she spoke of. The skirts of her cream dress rustled, and her dark curls bobbed under a simple wicker bonnet. The locket around her neck glinted in the sunlight. Joseph gazed at her and smiled.

'Not only are you a beautiful creature but charming and intelligent too.' He said. 'I must thank you again for accepting my offer to meet again. I was so captivated by your performance the other week.'

Maria looked away, 'Oh, people think I am fascinating but

truly, I am not. All I really seek is a life of contentment.' Her eyes drifted further into the distance. She had still not seen or heard from Buckley. A letter had arrived that morning and she had run down the stairs only to realise it had been for her father. She had waited to hear from him and even thought this time he would be true to his word. She felt foolish yet again. A tear formed in her eye, but she quickly wiped it away before smiling and turning to her new admirer, with whom she felt so at ease. They had talked and laughed on their meetings, and she felt like he was more of a friend. Perhaps this is what I should be looking for instead of the brooding and unpredictable Buckley, she thought.

Maria looked up at Hayne who continued to gaze at her, 'Yes, contentment is my desire too,' he agreed.

'Tell me of your plans in Cheltenham Mr Hayne. What brings you here from Staffordshire? I hear you might be joining the many investors in the town?'

'Oh yes, you have heard?' Joseph laughed. 'News travels fast here. Well, of course, Cheltenham is the ideal place for someone with fortune to spend some time researching opportunities.'

Maria looked up at her companion earnestly. 'How interesting. And what does your research tell you?'

Joseph touched his neatly tied neck collar with one hand and thought for a moment before he began, 'That Cheltenham continues to attract the great and good. I might be a young fellow, but I can spot an opportunity. In fact, I plan to invest in Mr Pitt's new zoological gardens. He has ambitious plans for his Pittville estate, and I intend to be part of it.' Joseph paused.

Maria nodded, 'I see. I have heard the Pittville rooms are rather grand, and that Mr Pitt has bigger plans. Let us walk Mr Hayne.' She took his arm and the pair strolled side-by-side further into the gardens. Joseph gave a slight skip as they went.

'Have you not visited? Oh, I must take you there! Quite an experience. I do admire Mr Pitt yes. I see myself becoming quite well-known in Cheltenham, just like him.' Joseph grinned at Maria who smiled in return. She liked his optimism and his boyish innocence. They walked further into the garden which became quieter. Joseph peered around him and then broke a momentary silence between them.

'Enough about my business interests, Miss Mount. How long are you to stay here? For the whole season?'

She smiled at him, 'Oh yes, I have a house here where my parents live. I will be here for performances until the end of the season.'

'And you must be used to many admirers?' Joseph stopped, turned, and looked searchingly into Maria's eyes. The actress blushed and looked away.

A couple stared at the pair as they passed and greeted them with a nod. Joseph gently touched Maria's elbow with his hand and led her deeper into the winding paths of the gardens. The fragrance of roses and jasmine followed them. Hetty stayed at a discreet distance as they entered a winding path off the main drive. The sound of the orchestra quietened further as the hedges deepened and after a short stroll, the pair sat on a bench.

Here Joseph turned to Maria and suddenly clasped her hands, 'I must...I must... declare my love, Miss Mount. In fact, as soon as I saw you on stage the other week, I knew I would make you my wife. I must further my suit and ask if you will permit me to visit your father. Will you say yes? Please will you allow me?'

Maria laughed, throwing her head back to reveal her pale smooth neck. Joseph frowned slightly but then leant in closer. 'Oh, you are divine!' he exclaimed. 'I know it seems rushed, but I am sure Miss Mount! I can offer you the life of contentment of which you spoke. I promise. I will give you everything and anything you might want. If you wish to continue on the stage, I would allow it. If you wanted to travel, we would do it. Anything, Miss Mount. Say yes and I will spend my life striving to make you the happiest and most content lady in the world.'

Maria grinned and gently brushed her lace gloved hand down the side of Joseph's face. His cheeks were flushed and his bright eyes gazed directly into hers.

She looked away, and when she spoke any laughter in her voice had vanished. 'Oh Mr Hayne, I am flattered really, but you must know that I have heard all this many times before. Despite my youth, I feel I am used to this attention. Perhaps I should spend my life as a spinster. There are plenty of unmarried ladies here in Cheltenham where the normal rules and regulations do not necessarily exist.' She laughed again but the ease of their earlier conversation had suddenly dissipated.

Joseph looked down for a moment before quickly lifting his gaze back to Maria. 'Of course, you are hesitant, and we have only just met. But let me endeavour to convince you. I admit, I have been seeking a wife these past few months. I have encountered many ladies who would seek to be betrothed to me. I have a vast fortune, not only from my Staffordshire estate but other holdings in many counties. Miss Mount, I can assure you of my steadfastness, my infatuation is of course, overwhelming, and I have never felt like this towards another.' He paused, still staring earnestly at her. 'Our meetings, our conversations. I have never felt so at ease with someone. If you would say yes, I would promise my loyalty and my life to you.'

Maria was quiet. She sighed and looked away. For so long her heart had been elsewhere. For so long she had been let down by a man who had promised her the world and yet never delivered. Here, now, she believed that this kind and earnest gentleman who looked at her with pleading eyes could offer her the life she craved.

She sighed again, 'You do not know everything about me and my past. I have had to create a life for myself; a very unconventional life.'

Joseph said nothing, but continued to gaze into Maria's eyes as they sat still, facing each other on the bench. Maria looked at this innocent man and thought of her long desire to be married to William Buckley. She felt a surge of anger towards her former lover. She thought of her desire to be reunited with her children and suddenly felt overwhelmingly protected, as if the future for her children would be secure with this young man of means. She clutched her locket, and a surge of happiness and hope caused her to place both hands on her heart before she burst out, 'I will allow it. For too long I have waited for such an offer, and I know you are sincere… but I must tell you–'

Before she could finish, Joseph had bounced up from his seat, sank down onto one knee and grasped her hand, kissing it on the back and front over and over. 'Oh, Miss Mount!' he cried, 'You make me the happiest man alive! I shall make arrangements at once. I shall write to your father and mother to arrange a visit and then I will explain that I desire to be united in marriage to their daughter! Oh Miss Mount, you are my love, and I will make you the happiest you have ever been!'

Maria laughed at Joseph's delight and when a tear sprang to her eye, she briefly tilted her head back. I will tell him everything, she thought. But not yet. She shook her head and smiled as she faced her husband to be.

Chapter 11

It was a rare afternoon when the reverend promised his wife and children a trip out to the countryside in their carriage. Filled with excitement at the prospect of an outing instead of Bible readings, lessons, and accompanying their parents to their various 'good works' around the town, the children had been running in and out of their father's study all morning. He had lowered his glasses and waved them out good-humoured-ly, and when noon came, he gathered his notes, smiled, and leapt out of his chair.

'Sarah! Harriet!' the reverend called the parlour maid and cook as he walked out into the parlour, put on a long brown coat over his breeches and white shirt and picked up a worn wooden walking stick by the door. His calls had alerted almost everyone in the house to attend: the children came running down the stairs followed by Elizabeth, while the maid came dashing from the kitchen with a small brown basket. The reverend beamed at them as they all started talking at once.

'Oh father, are we ready?' the children shouted.

'Francis, you're wearing breeches and not your robe?' Elizabeth looked wide-eyed at her husband.

'Sir, it's all ready!' Sarah said as she bustled in. 'Harriet has made her best lardy cake and you have some ham sandwiches and lemonade.'

'Lemonade!' Isobel and her brother Clarence chorused.

They ran to their father and hugged him. Elizabeth looked at her husband and beamed.

'Yes, lemonade and breeches my dears!' The reverend laughed, took the basket from Sarah, instructed his children to put on their coats, and led them out onto the drive and into his modest black carriage. The two horses yoked to the waiting carriage snorted, and the driver sat upright in his seat as the family emerged. Elizabeth, wearing a green high-waisted walking dress and a wicker bonnet, was helped up the step by her husband.

It was a fine day as the carriage travelled through Lansdown and onto the St. George's Road. It went onwards at a leisurely pace past the new free church in St Paul's, through the little village of Prestbury and then onto the approach of Cleeve Hill. The family passed an ancient farm as they crossed the parish boundary, and an old sheepdog ran to the gate, barking as the children waved from the carriage. The reverend and his wife smiled at each other and answered their children's questions with patience as the carriage started to climb the main route up to Cleeve Hill.

'Can we go all the way up the hill Father?'

'Will we be able to see everything from the top?'

'Will we be able to see your church from up there Father?'

'Mother, can we have the cake as soon as we stop?'

'We might not make it the full way up, but we will certainly get to a point where we can enjoy a magnificent view.' The reverend smiled.

When they had ascended about halfway up the rough track, the reverend hit the ceiling of the carriage with his walking stick and the vehicle came to a halt. The children bounded out with Elizabeth and the reverend following closely behind. They all stood gazing at the scene spread below them; like a map studded with woods, water, towns and villages and bounded by the hills of Malvern and South Wales. The reverend inhaled the country air deeply, closed his eyes and breathed a silent prayer of thanksgiving.

'Father, look, it's St Mary's!' his daughter proudly pointed her chubby finger in the direction of the town's first church. Its stout spire reached up solidly and reverently above the neighbouring buildings. The reverend smiled and then narrowed his eyes as he glanced towards Prestbury Manor below them. Beyond the manor, within a wide stretch of park, the reverend then spotted the race grandstand. He knew of its existence but had not been to see it. He shook his head, turned away and walked back to the carriage to retrieve the basket of treats.

Once the family were happily settled on a wide wicker mat, Elizabeth reached into the basket and brought out the sandwiches and lemonade. The children and their father cheered as she served them in little tin cups. Elizabeth watched her husband as he looked joyfully upon the children. She laughed to herself as his white shirt billowed out in the breeze and his soft brown hair fluffed out at the sides. She chuckled as he drank from his little tin mug of lemonade, realising she had never seen him looking quite so carefree.

In the next moment, the reverend had taken up his white handkerchief and started modelling shapes. First, he created a boat by folding the sides. His game required the children to guess the object as he acted out its movement. Next, he deftly modelled a replica church with a few twists of the fabric. The children laughed with glee as they tried to copy their father with handkerchiefs Sarah had packed for the picnic. Elizabeth laughed at the scene.

After an hour on the hill, the reverend rounded the children up and they bundled happily back into the waiting carriage. The horses which had been allowed to graze were retied and the vehicle set on its way back down the steep slope of Cleeve Hill. The afternoon was still sunny and warm, and the gentle rocking of the carriage sent the two children to sleep.

The reverend looked over at his wife, who sat with their son's head on her lap. 'You have made my life so full Elizabeth.' He said gently and smiled.

She beamed back at him. 'You make mine full too, my dear,' she replied. The couple sat in peaceful tranquillity and the journey gradually grew smoother as they came to the base of the hill and travelled alongside fields before arriving at the more populated village of Prestbury. They passed the King's Arms inn, rounded a corner, and then progressed onto a crossroads. Usually a quiet spot, the passengers were suddenly alerted to the driver shouting and the horses suddenly neighing. This was followed by a sharp jolt inside the carriage which sent the children flying across to the opposite seats and the peaceful scene was shattered.

Quick as a flash, the reverend poked his head outside the window with a fierce, 'What on earth!' And as soon as he looked, he saw a yellow high-topped fly speeding in the opposite direction.

'It nearly ran us off the track, Sir!' the driver cried. He bounced off his perch to the ground and the reverend swung open the carriage door and got out. The yellow carriage continued up the hill, paying no mind to the shock it had left in its wake.

'That is Colonel William Buckley.' The reverend whispered under his breath. 'The scoundrel.' His eyes narrowed as he gazed after the rapidly retreating vehicle. He returned to the carriage. Elizabeth was comforting the children who had been suddenly jolted from their slumbers. His family, so jovial a moment ago, were now looking at him with concern.

'What happened? Who was it?' Elizabeth ventured.

'It was Colonel Buckley. On his way back from the new Prestbury racecourse no doubt.'

'Who is Colonel Buckley?' The children chorused.

'No matter, my dears. No matter.' The reverend said soothingly, but shook his head to Elizabeth as the children turned to look out of the window. 'It is my job to drive this out; I know it will take time, but I am determined.' He said to Elizabeth in a low voice. 'These vain pleasures must end!'

Catching the tone of their father's voice, the children sat very still. All the excitement of the day had been extinguished. Elizabeth glanced tentatively at her husband to see that he had an earnest expression and was deep in thought. He knocked the roof of the carriage and they continued their journey home. As they passed the St. Paul's Free Church, a family of parishioners were standing outside when they spotted the reverend's carriage and began to wave. It was a man and woman and two children of similar age to the ones in the carriage. The family were dressed in clean but ragged clothes. The reverend, Elizabeth, and the children all looked out and waved back. The sight of the family briefly brought a smile to the reverend's face but then he spoke again in his usual serious tone.

'Why was it that during the Reform Bill, there was not the smallest of political outbursts amongst the lower classes of Cheltenham? Why is it that our walls were not placarded with inflammatory and seditious handbills, as in other towns, exciting the feeling of the populace against the Government? Not an act or outrage occurred.' The reverend paused and shook his head. 'My dear Elizabeth, I can say with certainty, that this is because there has been an interchange of sympathy between the rich and the poor, through the medium of charitable institutions like ours.'

Elizabeth looked briefly to her children who were still gazing out of the window, 'Husband, it is you who is behind all this. You created these institutions. But we have had a lovely day and we must not allow these vicious persons such as Buckley to disquiet us and distract us from our course.'

'Elizabeth, I persevere. It is my calling.' The couple stared at each other for a moment before the reverend reached out to hold his wife's waiting hand.

Chapter 12

The evening of the race ball was warm and still. As the guests arrived at the Old Prestbury Manor, a pale blue dusk was settling on the horizon and a full moon sat at the crest of Cleeve Hill. Swifts swooped and darted in the vast sky above Prestbury Park as insects danced and swarmed in the last evening heat of the late June day.

Carriages had pulled up outside the front of the manor and light from the grand arched doorway streamed onto the gravelled drive. Large windows revealed an oak panelled banquet hall inside and as Maria's fly carriage pulled up outside, she could see it was already full of people. She gasped at the size of the estate as she stepped out and looked up and around. The old manor looked even more magnificent in the evening. Its ivy-covered Cotswold stone walls were lit by small gas lamps at the sides of the driveway which ran all the way up to the moat encircling the manor. Its water reflected the brightness and beyond stretched the darkness of the new racecourse. Maria could only make out a few trees in the moonlight.

Behind the actress her party followed from the carriage: two friends from the theatre: Bess and Jerome, and Joseph, who she had decided to invite at the last minute. Their engagement was not yet formal; however, the pair had continued to promenade together most mornings. Of course, there will be a scandal, she thought as she stepped up to the huge arched entrance. Buckley will be here, but I will avoid him. She smiled to herself and felt a flash of excitement. *For once, he can wonder about me.*

The party was greeted by a smart butler in a black and white uniform who led them inside. He took Maria's cape to reveal a green silk opera cloak, the wide hood over her shoulders. Maria stood in the doorway and brushed her hand over a leafy plant. The grand entrance to Prestbury Manor was vast and held a great glass chandelier. Enormous plants reached the ceiling and a red carpeted central corridor led to a huge banquet hall. The walls were hung with landscape paintings in gilded frames, and a marble bust of a Roman emperor rested on a marble stand in an alcove. An oak staircase with ornately carved banisters rose from the centre of the reception hall and curved up to the rooms above.

Joseph, dressed smartly in a green tweed coat and breeches, stood proudly beside Maria and beamed at her as the party was escorted to the banquet hall by the butler, who left them on the threshold with a bow. The wood panelled room held another two huge chandeliers which dropped from two pendants in a decorated plaster ceiling. Within the hall, about one hundred people mingled as drinks were circulated on trays and a small orchestra played from a raised minstrels' gallery in the centre of the room. The women dazzled in evening dress and jewels and the men wore tweed, and as Maria and her party walked in, conversation almost stopped; those nearest to the group looked askance while those further away simply stared.

Maria knew that the crowd would be taking in Bess's mass of blonde hair and her tall and equally voluptuous figure. She was playing the nurse in the Cambray's Romeo and Juliet production, and while some of the guests had likely seen her onstage, Maria knew that Bess in her sweeping red dress was far more striking than in her dowdy nurse costume. While the tall and slim Jerome, who was playing Mercutio, wore any costume with stature and tonight stood proudly wearing a bright yellow jacket and flamboyant white shirt. Being recognised and talked about was nothing new to them. Maria smiled, bowed slightly and turned to her friends. In contrast to the poise of the actors, Joseph smoothed down his collar and looked about the room.

Before she could speak to them, Fulwar skipped across and gushed at his prestigious guest and her companions. His red breeches and blue jacket clashed. 'My dear, Miss Mount! I am so glad you could attend. I have so been looking forward to seeing you since the season started.' Her host held out his hands and then took her gloved hand and kissed it. 'I have been so busy with the race planning that I have not been able to get to the theatre, please forgive me. Mother has been and she says your performance was most commanding!' Fulwar's eyes fell on Bess, his gaze lingering as Maria laughed.

'Fulwar Chamberlayne, it has been some time. It is good to see you. Is your mother well?' The actress asked as she leaned closer to Joseph and took his arm.

Fulwar momentarily wrenched his gaze from Bess and ignoring Maria's question asked, 'And your esteemed friends here, are they all from the theatre?'

Maria smiled and gestured to the actors, 'Let me introduce my fellow performers Bess Boothy and Jerome D' Sule...'

Fulwar interrupted and smiled once more at Bess. 'Oh, Bess Boothy, what a fabulous name. Is it real?'

Bess smiled slowly as she looked him up and down and winked at him.

Fulwar gushed, 'Oh Bess, I'm glad you came. I think you'll no doubt brighten the place up...I...'

'I must introduce you to Mr Hayne here,' Maria interrupted, not wanting her guest to go ignored. 'He is a newcomer to Cheltenham and has never been to the races. I'm sure you will give him a little background?' Maria laughed again and turned to smile at Joseph who grinned at her and then at his host.

Fulwar laughed heartily and those nearby turned to look. He stepped closer to Joseph, 'Well, yes... I am very involved...

and we have this little party every year. It really is the start of the race events you know Mr Hayne. I will gladly tell you more about it later... but now, Miss Mount.' The host held out his hands in apology. 'I promised mother I would speak to her friends about the new racecourse. I will return very shortly. In the meantime, I believe there is a couple eager to make your acquaintance, a Mr and Mrs Harman.' He turned and gestured to a tall lady and a short man standing near an ornate stone fireplace. The pair smiled and bowed at Maria and Joseph before moving closer.

Maria smiled at the couple, and as they approached took the opportunity to look around the room. She noticed Bess and Jerome had now shifted towards a waiter carrying flutes of champagne. Her eyes scanned further and suddenly, she saw him. Buckley was dressed in cream breeches and a black jacket. He was deep in conversation with a similarly dressed tall blonde man and had seemingly not noticed her arrival. Buckley's head was bent towards his companion in easy confidence. Maria felt a rush of both anger and excitement, but quickly turned her head towards Joseph and the pair who had joined them.

The tall lady giggled, 'Oh, Miss Mount, it really is such a pleasure to meet you!' The couple were standing with their backs to Buckley and Maria could glance over the short man. Buckley had still not noticed her.

'Why thank you, Mrs Harman.' Maria turned and introduced Joseph who beamed. His confidence and friendliness were only found in young men who had been raised in the company of money and manners. It did not occur to him that he might be unwelcome in a new place. 'Is racing something which you follow avidly?' he asked, his eyes bright.

The lady laughed, 'Oh yes, of course, we have been attending the races since the start. It was up on the hills for years wasn't it dear?' She turned to Mr Harman who had said nothing but stood looking up at Maria with awe. She gave her husband a small nudge.

'Oh, yes, yes from the start, my dear,' he repeated.

The lady continued, 'We have even been out to watch it at Andoversford these last few years, but it was not the same. The turf up on the hill is better and you get to see the whole race. It will be interesting to see the new course. It has been personally mapped out by Colonel Buckley. He is behind us, you know?' the lady turned to point him out and raised her eyebrows.

Maria smiled and took the opportunity to look over again at the man she felt both anger and adoration for. 'He does keep himself busy.' She muttered. Her gaze lingered and for a moment, Buckley leaned back in laughter. He then surveyed the room with all the satisfaction of the host.

Maria's gaze returned to the couple who simultaneously nodded in agreement.

The lady then moved in closer and spoke in whispered tones, 'Of course, you know what happened seven years ago, with the grandstand? Arson, many said, but it was never proven. The reverend's followers called it an act of God.'

Maria nodded. She knew the story, as she knew most of Cheltenham's stories. But at this moment all she could think about was Joseph's proposal and her desire for Buckley to know about it. Was it revenge she sought? She wasn't sure. Perhaps she secretly hoped that Buckley would drop everything and marry her instead and that, at last, she could bring her children home. She clutched the locket around her neck and gazed again around the room.

Across the grand banquet hall, Lord Croft was standing with his back against a tapestry, speaking to two elderly men who nodded with interest as he spoke. 'It will be a quite a moment to see the races return to the town. Although, I did enjoy the Andoversford site for a while. More rugged I thought, and I did like the little inn which we used to go to.'

One of the men was drawing a circle in the air with his finger, 'Yes, but you could not see the riders all the way round the course. Do you remember Dick Oliver's colourful capers?'

Lord Croft guffawed, 'I am well aware of Oliver's dealings. Which caper are you recalling? He might be a brilliant jockey, but I hear he is in prison now. Bad debt apparently.'

The elderly man nodded, 'Well, once it was said he was riding the Andoversford chase in a January meet. There were two circuits of the course to complete, and so confident was he in his belief that no one in the stand could see much through the snow, he stopped his horse first time round and took shelter behind a haystack. As the toiling field loomed up again several minutes later, Oliver remounted and re-joined the race – in the lead of course.'

All three men laughed loudly, and Maria glanced around as others in the room looked over to the group. The couple were still talking, and Joseph gladly listened while Maria noticed Bess talking to Fulwar who quickly moved his hand to the base of her friend's back as they left the room. Maria smiled to herself as Fulwar glanced back over his shoulder with a small smirk on his face.

'Miss Mount!' Suddenly Buckley was standing before the group, looking from Maria's face to Joseph's as he boomed his greeting and beamed a wide smile. Mr and Mrs Harman inched back to the fireplace to watch the encounter as others in the room turned to look. Buckley nodded slowly and there was an awkward pause before Maria offered her hand.

'Colonel Buckley. Let me introduce you to Mr Joseph Hayne of Staffordshire.'

'Welcome to Cheltenham Mr Hayne.' Buckley bowed slightly as he looked the younger man up and down.

'Thank you. It is a pleasure to meet someone of such esteem. I hear you have quite an involvement with the racecourse?' Joseph put out his hand, but Buckley failed to take it. The former momentarily looked down at the ground but regained his composure.

'Yes, yes, ha…' Buckley now looked coolly from Maria to her young companion who he stood nearly half a foot above. 'And what are your plans here, Mr Hayne?'

Joseph puffed up his chest, 'Well, many... in fact, it is my desire to invest in Mr Pitt's new scheme, have you heard? Very ambitious plans for zoological gardens.'

Buckley raised his eyebrows at Maria and suppressed a sneer. 'I have heard about some mad plans in the south of town at The Park but not of plans in Pittville. It seems everybody and anybody is developing a spa here, or a pleasure ground there. I for one doubt it will last. If you want my advice Mr Hayne, these men have simply got lucky. Their involvement with property and land transactions have led them to believe they can engage in land speculation themselves, but I doubt if they really know anything about owning land or how to manage it at all. I would steer clear of that Mr Pitt and his plans if I were you.' He waved his arm dismissively.

Joseph stared at Buckley, speechless. His chest had now de-flated, the grin wiped off his face. Maria looked from one man to the other and frowned, 'I admire anyone with an ambitious plan to better society.' She said, laying a protective hand on Joseph's arm with a smile.

*

Outside the manor Fulwar had sensed his opportunity to gain more knowledge of Bess Boothy. Having ducked out of the party, the pair now dashed like fugitives up the gravelled driveway and across to the moat, stepping gingerly along its spongy side to the little wooden bridge.

'Oh, I know you were game from the moment you looked at me, Miss Boothy. And that name!'

The vast Prestbury Park lay out before them. The moonlight afforded enough vision for the giggling pair to scuttle down a steep slope to the flat land below. It was soft and slightly muddy but neither cared as Bess simply laughed and fell into her companion. Fulwar grabbed her around the waist and pulled her voluptuous form towards him. 'Oh, you are a fine filly indeed.' He kissed her quickly and sloppily on the mouth and she responded to his urges with groans. Her arms clamped around his head and the pair almost seemed to be wrestling as they came down heavily onto the soft ground of the racecourse.

'It's like that is it, Bessy Boothy? I thought you only wanted to see the racecourse?' Fulwar laughed as he lay flat on the ground. Bess silenced him with another open-mouthed kiss as she held his arms above his head and mounted him. She lifted her skirts and flung her head back as she ground her hips over his groin.

'Stay there.' She whispered as she swiftly moved to open his breeches to work her hand in expert skill over his manhood.

'Oh ride me Bessy, you naughty girl!' Fulwar groaned with pleasure as the actress rocked against him. As the pair reached the height of their fumbling pleasures, almost as soon as the encounter had started, the darkness beyond absorbed the sounds of their frolicking while the lights of Prestbury Manor twinkled just beyond the steep slope they had tumbled down.

*

Back in the ballroom, Joseph had found his voice while Buckley had assumed an air of indifference to the young investor, who was oblivious to any challenge, 'Well, strong words Sir, but I...' Before Joseph could continue, Fulwar returned. He was smoothing down his floppy hair and it was only Buckley who noticed the mud on his host's jacket. Bess scuttled in a few moments behind with a smirk on her face. Fulwar grinned at Buckley as he approached and slapped his friend on the back. He turned to Joseph and grabbed his elbow.

'Mr Hayne, I must show you the map of the racecourse! I have been showing mother's friends and they were delighted.

Even gave me some tips. Come, come through.' Fulwar half dragged the young man from Maria's side. The actress was left standing alone in front of Buckley who stared at her.

Maria sighed and rolled her eyes. 'You didn't have to challenge Mr Hayne.'

'I don't think he noticed, Miss Mount.'

Maria winced. 'I have not heard from you since the day we met at the Montpellier Spa.' Maria searched his eyes for any signs of affection, but he grinned, looked down and then put his arms behind his back.

'I have been very busy. As you know. I have been involved in the races here. But how have things been with you Miss Mount? How are the shows? Sell outs? I will be along again the night before the races as everything will be set up by then. It seems you have been busy too.' Buckley nodded to where Joseph had been standing.

Maria frowned and lowered her voice; her normally powerful presence felt suddenly small. 'A note from you would have been the least you could have sent. I have had many bouquets and notes from admirers these past few weeks. But, from you? Nothing.'

'Well Maria, I observe that you brought an admirer here tonight and you seem to be enjoying his company?' Buckley huffed.

Maria stayed silent and looked into Buckley's eyes. He avoided her look, his eyes searching the room, rolling slightly before he looked back at her. She remained silent.

Buckley suddenly laughed, 'Now, I must be going.' He went to move away but Maria clasped his hand.

'William, will I see you soon? I must tell you, I am being courted. In fact, I have had a proposal of marriage.'

Buckley stopped, moved back and looked down at Maria. His face scrunched in annoyance and he moved nearer to her again.

'By whom?' he asked slowly. Buckley's lips pursed and his

strong brows drew together. People in the room were now looking at them. Some were whispering behind their hands. Maria looked around quickly to see if Joseph was still in the room and then looked defiantly back at Buckley.

'By the young gentleman you just met, Mr Hayne. He wishes to look after me.' Maria gushed out her words and suddenly felt pathetic. She wanted to stop Buckley walking away by any means possible. She had longed to be with this man ever since she had first met him ten years ago. For him to marry her and value her, and for him, the father of her beloved children to enable her to bring them home to raise as a family. She pushed back a lump in her throat and took a deep breath.

Buckley stood and looked at her. His eyes narrowed as he moved towards her and whispered, 'I see... and are you going to accept?'

Maria looked up into his eyes which had blackened. His nostrils flared, and his lips were set in a grim line. Then suddenly his eyes were cold, unfeeling. She knew this look well and felt foolish for allowing him to follow her into the basement the other day when his eyes had been full of longing – for one thing.

'I have.' she whispered. 'I am to be no man's mistress.'

Without a parting nod or word, Buckley turned on his heel and strode from the hall.

Maria was left standing by the fireplace. She put one hand on her stomach and reached out with the other to steady herself on the mantle. The tall lady and her short companion stared at the actress and smiled timidly; their eyes wide.

Chapter 13

The Barnett's Riding School also served as the Town Hall and was the venue for the monthly evening meeting of the Cheltenham Benevolent Society. The long, white-washed room had benches temporarily laid out and seated along them were society members who quietly chattered and cast glances at the table at the front of the room. Behind the table stood the black-robed Reverend Francis Cole who was unclasping his large cylindrical metal carrying case and extracting a rolled piece of paper: his notes for the evening's talk.

'Good evening, ladies and gentlemen.' The reverend nodded and looked about the room as the society members came to a complete hush. He looked behind him, gathered his black robe and then sat on a high-backed chair behind the table. A small elderly lady in the front row with thinning grey hair and a bird-like face shifted a little in her seat. An even older gentleman next to her had closed his eyes and folded his arms, while a thin, earnest looking man next to him leant forward in contrast.

The reverend cleared his throat and held his notes up slightly. He then reached down for his glasses and placed them on the end of his nose, 'We all know what is being celebrated this very evening, and I will soon come to talk of upcoming events. But first, I would like to celebrate a victory of our own. As we all know, our latest infant school was opened in Wynnstay House some weeks ago. The Cheltenham Infant School is now full of the children of those hard-working members of our town.'

A murmur of approval rose among the benches and the reverend paused and smiled before he continued, 'We now have the means of introducing not less than eight hundred children of the most respectable persons into educational institutions in the town. I can continue to recommend our schools here in Cheltenham and vouch that this is a safe place to which to send our young.' There was another murmur of approval.

'However...' The reverend paused, clasped his hands and looked about him, his face stern. 'Deeply interested as I am in promoting the increasing prosperity of this highly favoured place, I want to remind you that the races commence next week and we as clergy are doing our upmost to keep people from going to them. My tracts are being distributed and published and sermons are preached in all the churches. We will provide all those school children who do not go to the races with buns and tea on the Well Walk, and I am pleased to add that we now have a number of highly prominent members of society who now stand by us. Our cause only gains year on year.'

'Hear! Hear!' the bird-like lady called, and the gathered members nodded and shuffled in their seats. The earnest man nodded his head vigorously while the older gentleman opened and closed his eyes.

The reverend pressed down his notes. His voice was steady, but he deliberately looked at each person in the room as he spoke, 'So, I would encourage you to remind our fellow citizens that they must choose between the advantage held out to them by the one part or the other.'

The thirty or so society members in the room came to a complete hush. Even the elderly gentleman opened his eyes briefly as the reverend continued, 'If people are persuaded that our well-earned reputation for successful education is the greatest present attraction to our town, then we must have down with the cruelties, the gambling and the concomitant debaucheries of all sorts; or if people choose to multiply our races and increase their criminal amusements, then shut up our schools and colleges.' The reverend held his hands out wide, palms up, like a set of scales, 'The two things are incompatible. Determine which you will have, and the parents and friends of eight hundred youths will know how to act – the races can no longer be tolerated among us.' The reverend paused and the members started to shift in their seats and murmur.

The reverend raised his hands and resumed when the murmurs died. 'I know this is not our usual topic of benevolence, but tonight I wanted to reiterate my strength of feeling that we need to be united against this evil which pervades our good society.' He cleared his throat, 'As we know, the races were initiated before I settled in the town in the year of 1827, and by then, they had reached a pitch of abomination. Cleeve Down and its various approaches by day and night presented scenes of shameless and disgusting debauchery, disgraceful even to a heathen land. I saw many wagon loads of men and women pass the house where I then lived in a filthy state of intoxication, singing songs and uttering profaneness of the lowest description.' The reverend paused and shook his head as the audience looked on, enraptured.

'The evils were so great and so patent to all, that as soon as possible after I became incumbent of the parish, I commenced an annual denunciation from the pulpit. My efforts were ridiculed, and I brought on myself bitter persecution.' The members muttered and nodded their heads again before the reverend stretched out his hands, 'But, by God's grace I have persevered each succeeding year to reduce the number of respectable supporters of the races. These efforts have so far told upon the races and they have so palpably fallen off. But now an attempt is being made to revive them by bringing them down into the valley nearer the town and they are to be held in Prestbury Park. Their plan may go ahead this year, but

I am determined that it will not continue to succeed. And this intolerable nuisance will be finally removed.'

'Hear! Hear!' the bird-like lady called again, and the earnest man nodded vigorously as a chorus of other 'Hear! Hears!' echoed. The reverend now raised his hand and pointed his finger in the air as he continued:

'If the character of the races is undergoing a gradual change and if they are not opposed at once and resisted by the respectable inhabitants, all the abomination of the original races may soon be inflicted upon us. We know of at least two deaths caused by previous year's sport, one resulting in a charge of manslaughter, for which three unhappy wretches are now incarcerated, besides several accidents in broken limbs, which have all been as much as possible hushed up over the years.'

The reverend looked out at the gathering as the listeners continued to nod and murmur. The elderly gentleman closed his eyes again. The meeting continued in practical terms with the distribution of duties for the Buns and Tea event and notes for the school volunteers. When the meeting came to an end the society members dispersed after a few brief interactions with each other and the reverend. The benches were replaced by two gentlemen who stayed behind to help and who made sure to turn off the gas lights and lock the large double doors to the riding school. The gentlemen bid farewell to the reverend as he turned to walk the half mile to his Lansdown House residence while the pair went in the opposite direction to the high street.

The night was still, and with a full moon, the streets were easy to navigate. The reverend always walked home from his daily visits to St Mary's and from any meetings he had in town. He always carried his long metal carrying case and sometimes even his large Bible. Tonight, he had only his carrying case as he strode along the road. It swished against his cloak in time to his stride. He passed some newly built townhouses, continued on across the now silent promenade and then began the gentle climb into Lansdown: a less populated area with fields and occasional large villas along the route.

Once up the hill into Lansdown, the reverend turned a corner into a crescent. Its four-storey houses of Cotswold stone stood brightly in the moonlight. Turning again into a shortcut down an alleyway between the grand houses, he walked slower. The light hardly penetrated here and the reverend had to find his way along the path by touch and memory.

He sometimes sang hymns as he walked, but tonight he simply listened; the only sound was his footsteps and the swishing of his metal case which hung slightly awkwardly across his body with a leather strap. As he turned into Lansdown Road, his surroundings seemed quieter still and, despite it being a mild night, the reverend shivered. He stopped. His skin prickled as he had the feeling of being watched. He stood still and the case swishing ceased as he held the vessel tight to his body. The sudden screech of an owl hooting in the distance made him jump and he looked behind him before setting off again on the final stretch to his house. He could see the welcoming turrets of his grand home in the moonlight, and he thought happily of Elizabeth, who would be waiting up for him while their children were snug in their beds.

But then suddenly, he heard footsteps other than his own. He could hear them growing faster and closer. The reverend stopped. He looked around, scrutinising the shadows. Nothing there. He was not a man to be frightened easily, but all the same he crossed the road. He increased his pace and slowly moved his hands so they were on both ends of his carrying case. If he was approached, he would wield it as a weapon. His heart was beating as he looked wildly about him. Was that the shadow of a man behind? He hurried back over the road to reach his gateposts. Once inside his driveway, the reverend looked up at the light in his bedroom window, released his grip on the metal case and quickly removed a key from his pocket. The key dropped to the ground in his haste, and he bent to fumble for it in the dark. He was sure he could still hear footsteps, but now picking up the key and without turning back, he did not dare a glance behind him. Looking frantically ahead into his moonlit walled garden he reached the doorway and thrust the key into the lock, stepping gratefully into the safety of his own parlour. Quickly locking and bolting the door behind him, the reverend leaned against it. He was breathing heavily and his hands were trembling, his heart pounding in his chest. Here he stood for a while before shaking his head and taking a deep breath. He slowly removed his carrying case, placed it on a small table at the side of the parlour and then ascended the stairs for bed, resolving not to worry Elizabeth by telling her about the incident.

Chapter 14

On this July morning at Deanswood Villa, Mr Mount was as usual sat with his wife in the drawing room. His shifting eyes scanned the *Cheltenham Chronicle* which he held in one hand while, in the other, he twisted a piece of gold brocade which had come loose from his purple cloak. Mrs Mount sat opposite on her cushioned sofa. She leaned forward to a small round table where she was carefully placing some playing cards in a line.

Mr Mount gave a snort of a laugh, 'A lot about the upcoming races here. Some small mention of Maria at the race ball the other evening, and it appears the Reverend Cole has published one of his letters to the people of Cheltenham again.'

Mrs Mount looked up, 'Oh yes? What are they saying about Maria?'

'Oh, it's just a list of those attending... a long list of county families were in attendance, and many people of fortune. I see Miss Mount was with a Mr Hayne. Ah, the report here describes him... he seems to have most engaging manners... some charm in his face.'

'And why weren't we invited?' his wife asked sharply and frowned.

Mr Mount snorted again. 'For the same reasons we weren't invited to balls in Plymouth dear: we're neither respectable nor fashionable enough. Besides, I wouldn't want to go. I'm too old now to preen and puff up all those in society who think they are better than me.' He looked up for a moment, shook his head and then returned his gaze to the Chronicle.

'And the Reverend Cole? What does his letter say?' Mrs Mount picked up the cards and shuffled them as Hetty entered the room.

'A gentleman caller for Mr and Mrs Mount, Sir.'

Mr Mount laughed, 'A gentleman caller? Whatever does he want? Tell him I am not at home. Maria is upstairs, call her down Hetty.'

Hetty bobbed her head and suppressed an excited smile, 'Ah, no Mr Mount, the gentleman requests an audience with you only, Sir, but it is about Miss Mount. It is a Mr Hayne from Staffordshire.'

Mr Mount rolled his eyes, 'Ah, well, I see... that sort of gentleman caller.' He turned to his wife. 'Not the first to come courting our Maria.' He chuckled. 'Call him in.'

Hetty turned, left the room and after a moment, a young man stepped through the door of the drawing room and stood at the threshold twisting his hat nervously in his hands.

'Mr Joseph Hayne, Sir, Madam.' Hetty gave an awkward curtsy and retreated.

Mr Mount stood up, his long cloak open to reveal a black frilled shirt and black breeches. Joseph bowed to his host and Mr Mount moved forward, grabbed the visitor's hand and shook it vigorously.

'Mr Hayne, a pleasure I am sure!'

Mrs Mount stayed in her seat, the cards now stacked on the small table. She smiled and nodded at the gentleman as she looked him up and down.

'The pleasure is all mine, Mr and Mrs Mount.' Joseph turned to the lady and then began to shift from foot to foot; his face flushed. 'I am here to make a request Sir, and would be obliged if I could make that request with you in private.' Joseph bowed again, glancing and smiling at Mrs Mount.

Mr Mount nodded slowly and gestured out of the room, 'Of course, young man. Let us go into my office.'

The office at Deanswood Villa was at the back of the house overlooking the garden. Its large window looked out at the willow tree: its delicate branches swayed in the gentle summer breeze. A large oak desk in front of the window was covered in papers and newspaper clippings. Joseph observed a bookcase next to the desk and several playbills framed on the walls. He glanced at one which had browned with age which read 'The Playbill' at the top with, 'The Plymouth Theatre' at the bottom. Joseph quickly read, 'The nautical drama of the Blue Anchor,' before he turned to face Mr Mount who had sat back on a large worn leather-bound chair behind the desk and was beaming at the young man's interest in the wall frames.

'Perhaps my daughter has told you I was known as a great actor in my day?' Mr Mount asked as he gestured to the opposite seat.

'Ah, no she did not say Mr Mount,' Joseph nodded back at the playbills before shuffling from foot to foot and finally sitting down.

His host frowned momentarily and then spread his hands wide on the desk. 'Well. I have welcomed many fine gentlemen here. What is it you wanted to speak to me about in private young man?'

Joseph put his hat on the desk and cleared his throat, 'Mr Mount, Sir. I would very much like to make the intentions for my visit very clear from the start. I have been very anxious to find a suitable bride and I would count myself the most fortunate of men if you would consent to my marriage to your daughter.'

'Ah.' Mr Mount smiled at the young man in front of him. He lifted his hands, put them behind his head and leaned back in his chair. 'And how long have you known my daughter Mr Hayne?'

Joseph looked down at the desk again and then grinned back, 'Oh, I have known her long enough to know that she would make me very happy, very happy indeed, Sir. And I could provide her with all the love and security she desires. I met her at the start of this season and we have been on a number of promenades since – chaperoned of course.' Joseph explained hastily.

Mr Mount leaned forward; his hands were now clasped together. 'I see, well, as we are being very clear. I must tell you that my daughter is engaged to Colonel Buckley and has been for many years, and if and when this relationship is finally broken off, I am sure you will be in with a chance.'

He stared at Joseph who opened his mouth in shock, his flushed cheeks suddenly pale as he swayed slightly in his seat and then steadied himself with his hand on the desk. Leaning back in his chair shaking his head, Joseph asked with a shaking voice, 'I must ask Mr Mount, are you sure? I... I am aware she has a great number of admirers. But... but... Miss Mount would surely have informed me of a current union when I asked for her hand in marriage and expressed my desire to visit to your good self.' He thought for a moment. 'Was this not a prior engagement?'

Mr Mount sat perfectly still, his hands still clasped together. He affected a sober expression, paused a moment longer for dramatic effect and then turned his mouth upward into a slight smile before saying, 'I can assure you that this is very much a current engagement.'

Joseph remained wide-eyed and speechless. He then turned to face the wall of playbills. 'I...I did not know of this union.' He finally repeated softly as he shook his head.

Mr Mount sat back and frowned, 'Oh my dear young fellow, have you not been informed of Buckley and his set? I imagine being from Staffordshire you are not aware...' his voice tailed off as he pondered to himself.

Joseph turned his face back to Mr Mount. His face now flushed again and he raised his voice, 'Yes, I have encountered the fellow and found him rather condescending... I see now how he spoke to me...'

Mr Mount waved his hand and interrupted, 'You have an estate in the county of Staffordshire you say? As you are asking for my daughter's hand in marriage, I must ask what annual income she could expect.' Mr Mount twisted his head to the side and looked at Joseph from the corner of his eye. The young man was looking down at the desk again, but then seemed to collect himself, took a deep breath and hit the desk with a sudden slap of his hand.

'Mr Mount, I can assure you that if I married your daughter she would be looked after. I have a sizable income of over twelve thousand per annum which would undoubtedly keep her in comfort.'

Mr Mount's eyes glistened. He smiled and then raised his hand. 'Mr Hayne, I am grateful for your openness, but let me once again be frank. I have heard it all before. Security is what we want for Maria, and we of course have to consider our own futures.' He nodded sagely. 'My daughter would want myself and Mrs Mount kept in the manner we have become accustomed, you understand?'

Joseph spluttered, 'Well, with respect Mr Mount, you have just informed me of a good reason not to pursue your daughter.'

Mr Mount interrupted again and spoke firmly, 'If you're not interested in what I have to propose, you can leave now young man.'

Joseph looked down at the desk momentarily and shifted in his seat, 'I would like to hear what you have to propose.' He started to nod in time with Mr Mount who now sat forward and lowered his voice.

'If I was to ensure a clear path for you to marry my daughter, with no *obstacles*, this would require my time and negotiation with certain *obstacles*... and... this of course would incur costs, you understand Mr Hayne?'

Joseph nodded again and hesitated. He shuffled his feet and looked down at the desk again before looking up. 'You are offering to remove the obstacle of Colonel Buckley? But what if Maria has already rebuffed him? Is she here? Can I speak with her?'

'No, you cannot.' Mr Mount raised his voice slightly and stared at Joseph. 'My daughter, along with myself and Mrs Mount, are seeking someone who is sure about a betrothal. You cannot expect an actress to be without a past, dear fellow. You either want to marry her, or not. Whatever the *obstacle*.' He threw his hands up for dramatic effect.

There was an awkward silence before Joseph sighed and answered slowly, 'I must speak to my solicitor on matters of this nature.' He gazed at the playbills and seemingly spoke to himself. 'Although, I have never encountered this sort of matter.' Hayne scratched his head while Mr Mount sat back in his chair and watched before answering confidently.

'You have never encountered a lady like Maria before I imagine either, Mr Hayne?'

There was another silence as Joseph looked at his host and then beyond him, through the window behind to the swaying willow tree. Suddenly, he banged the table with his fist again and jumped up out of his seat to stand.

'Whatever it takes Mr Mount. I would do anything to marry your daughter.' His face was elated for a moment and then he frowned. 'If you can assist with the removal of any... obstruction, I would certainly reimburse you for your time and effort on this matter.'

'I prefer my costs upfront, you understand? And I was thinking along the lines of...' Mr Mount smiled as he reached for a pen and scribbled a figure on a piece of paper on the desk. He turned it around towards Joseph who picked it up, raised his eyebrows, nodded again and looked up.

'Whatever it takes Mr Mount – you shall receive this sum first thing tomorrow, of course, if you can guarantee a smooth path for Maria and I to marry? Do I have your full support and blessing in this union?'

Mr Mount laughed, stood up and moved around the desk to shake Joseph's hand.

The young man stood still, but Mr Mount leaned his face towards him and spoke softly, 'My man, you have my full support and blessing to marry Maria. I can assure you that this union will be of the upmost benefit to my daughter, and I will personally take care of any *obstacles* to this marriage.'

Joseph now danced from foot to foot, 'Oh Sir, I am most grateful. Might I also ask your permission to escort your good self and Mrs Mount to the theatre and to tender you in my private box?'

'It would be our pleasure.' Mr Mount's eyes gleamed as Joseph bowed.

'And might I ask permission to speak with Miss Mount now?' Joseph bowed again.

'Of course, I'll get the maid to call her down.' Mr Mount waved his hand flamboyantly, gathered his cloak around him and strode out of the room.

*

Joseph stood where he had been instructed to wait in the garden next to the summerhouse. The small wooden structure had three sides with the open front facing the willow tree. Inside the little house there was a small metal bench with a blue and red embroidered cushion perched in the middle.

'Mr Hayne!' the young gentleman turned at the sound of Maria's voice. She looked as radiant as ever, he thought. She was wearing a simple pale lilac muslin gown, her bosom heaved as she skipped along the lawn towards him. Her uncovered hair was in a neat, braided coronet. She looked the perfect picture of beauty. Joseph blushed and sighed to himself as she grasped his hand in hers.

'Miss Mount, I have been with your father...' he hesitated.

'I hear, and we are to be married!' Maria held both of his hands tighter and then rested her head on his chest. Joseph kissed the top of her head and closed his eyes.

'My love yes…But I must just ask you. Is your former romantic involvement to Colonel Buckley now dissolved?'

Maria looked up. Her large brown eyes filled with tears. 'My father told you about him?'

'Yes, my love. I… I would be a fool to believe you have not had past suitors, but I wish you had been honest with me about your former engagement. But my love for you is so…' his face suddenly clouded. 'But, that man… so very arrogant and forceful…goodness knows what you saw in him. You must make it clear to him; send him a note, telling him that you are engaged to me.'

Maria shook her head and sighed. 'I have informed him about your proposal already. It is over with him. My future lies with you, and I want for the entire world to be your wife.' She put her head on his chest again and Joseph wove his arms around her.

'Oh my love!' he kissed her hair again. 'You make me the happiest man alive!' His hands moved to Maria's waist as she lifted up her head and he kissed her softly on the lips. His lips closed, she felt gentleness as he lingered, but as his hands remained firmly on her waist she did not think she would lose herself in passion. He kissed her only for a moment before drawing back his head and gazing down into her eyes. She felt safe.

Maria held her locket and closed her eyes. 'Joseph, I must tell you about…'

'Maria! My dearest daughter!' Mr Mount strode into the garden with Hetty scurrying behind, precariously balancing an open bottle of champagne and flutes on a tray. Mrs Mount followed behind at a leisurely pace.

'Let us raise a glass to this union!' Mr Mount reached the couple and removed a glass from the tray, holding a flute first out to Joseph and then to Maria. The young man beamed at his bride to be. Maria took a sip from her glass and smiled back.

Chapter 15

It was an unusually cold night for July. The reverend was at home in Lansdown House and sitting on the north side of the grand building in the drawing room. He shivered as he fleetingly looked at the fireplace but quickly dismissed any thought of lighting it in the middle of summer.

The room was large, or at least large enough for the many meetings he held at his home for his Bible readings and updates on charitable works and benevolence. It had a grand stone carved fireplace, and the mantle above held a great mirror framed with extravagant gold leaf. A grandfather clock stood by the door, its methodical ticking resounding throughout the room. Paintings, mainly of pastoral scenes, adorned the walls and there was also a strikingly large portrait of the reverend depicting him standing in St Mary's Church with his pulpit behind him. The reverend's round, handsome face stared out of the picture at the real reverend who was seated in a comfortable armchair. He was wearing a burgundy dressing gown and his old pair of slippers. His gold spectacles were perched on his nose, and he looked at the piece of paper he held aloft and then down at his lap at a long list of notes.

The reverend rubbed his head and muttered to himself. Elizabeth and the children were upstairs getting ready for bed. He smiled to himself as he thought of his little ones being tucked up. He then gathered the papers up, heaved himself out of the chair and deposited them on a nearby squat table.

Just then, there was a knock at the open door as the reverend's grey haired and red-faced cook Harriet entered the room. She stood at the threshold holding a large basket under her arms.

The reverend frowned and waved his hand in the direction of the cook. 'Oh Harriet, you know I'm making preparations to receive a large missionary party at dinner tomorrow, and I have to attend two important meetings. I really cannot be disturbed.'

The cook smiled proudly. She looked down at the basket which, due to its weight, she now shifted round to the front to hold with both hands, 'But master, some kind friend has heard you are holding a missionary dinner and has sent you this fish. I thought I would bring it to you to open. There must be a lot of fish master, for the basket is so very heavy.'

The reverend frowned again momentarily as he remembered his walk home the other evening. He then softened and smiled at his faithful servant, beckoning her forward. 'Oh, bring it over then, let's have a look.'

Harriet walked further into the room. The reverend cleared his notes from the table and directed the basket to be placed before him. It was an ordinary rectangular brown wicker fish basket. It had two small holes at the top and a wide leather strap across the middle, with two smaller straps at the side to hold it in place. The cook stared and clasped her hands in anticipation as her master reached for both sides of the vessel and hastened to open it.

'It is a late hour for a delivery, is it not Harriet?' The reverend observed as he fumbled with the straps which had been pulled tightly in place.

'It is Sir, but you are always getting gifts.' She smiled and stood near, peering on expectantly. But as the reverend undid the straps and lifted the lid, she immediately recoiled and shrieked in horror as her master jumped back from the basket.

Instead of fish, the basket contained the body of a baby. The child was loosely swaddled in a dirty blanket, with a little grey lace cap upon its head. It was curled into the foetal position; its miniature hands touching, and its tiny feet tucked in. Its face looked peaceful. The little were eyes shut as if sleeping, but the lips were blue and the skin had a chalky tinge.

The reverend stared while his cook, her face ashen, was the first to speak as she staggered backwards, 'Oh, my, who did this? Why? Is the poor thing alive?' her voice reached a shriek.

The reverend shook himself and quickly leaned over the basket to press his fingers to the infant's forehead and then to its neck, just beneath the jaw. He felt no pulse, just smooth, cold skin. The poor child could not have been more than nine months old and apparently not long dead.

'Oh, shut it up again Master.' Harriet shrieked again and at that moment the parlour maid came rushing in. Elizabeth came running down the stairs with the children following close behind her.

'Elizabeth!' The reverend turned from the basket and shouted. 'Take the children upstairs at once!' His wife froze and stared at the basket. Standing at the threshold of the room, she didn't see inside it but quickly followed her husband's orders, turned, and bustled her children out of the room.

'But father?' they called back. 'What is it?' Elizabeth shushed them and gathered them away, looking back at the door to the drawing room as they climbed the stairs. Sarah approached the table and put her hands to her mouth in shock as she saw the little child in the basket. No one spoke and the three stared at the child for a moment.

'There is something on the child's hand.' Sarah pointed suddenly. The reverend leaned into the vessel again. There was what appeared to be a note crudely attached with string to the poor child's finger. With trembling hands, the reverend reached inside the basket and retrieved the small rolled up parchment. He slowly undid the string that tied it, opened it up and read aloud in a quiet but trembling voice, 'Behold thy likeness.'

Both Harriet and Sarah stood with their mouths open. They stared at the reverend who held the note carefully between his thumb and forefinger and brought it close to his face before holding it up to the light and turning it around.

'How did the basket arrive, Harriet?'

Harriet continued to stare at the basket with her hand held to her forehead, 'Master, it was received by Sarah in the parlour. I heard a man's voice, but then she brought it into the kitchen and said it was fish sent from Birmingham. I will take it away, and you will never hear anything more about it.'

'No, Harriet that will not do. There are plenty who know about it already. The wretched creatures who have sent me this know of it, the Devil knows of it, and happily God knows of it. You must not do that; we must not hide it.' He said firmly.

The reverend returned the note carefully to the basket and looked up at the parlour maid. The girl had tears in her eyes and was shaking her head. 'Now Sarah, describe the man who delivered the basket. This diabolical act...'

'Sir,' Sarah started to sob. 'It was just a delivery man...he was... it was dark... I have never seen him before...but he just said, "For the Reverend Cole." I took the basket from him and brought it inside. Oh master, have I done anything wrong?' She continued to sob uncontrollably.

'No, no of course not.' He turned to both of his servants. 'Neither of you have done anything wrong at all. It is whoever sent this to me who has done wrong. Who would commit such a terrible crime? Do they hope to destroy my name?' The reverend shook his head, paced the floor, and then turned back to the basket. He tenderly covered the little infant with the flimsy cotton cloth, touched the baby on the head and closed his eyes before muttering a short prayer. He then closed the lid carefully and retied the straps.

He looked up again and nodded to the cook. 'I tell you what you can do Harriet. It is too late now to call the constable, so I have blessed the poor wretch. You must put it down in the cellar and lock it up till tomorrow, for I have too much upon my mind this evening to attempt to think of it.'

'Yes Sir.' Harriet gathered herself, and nodding to Sarah to follow, picked up the basket and carried it out of the room. The reverend sighed heavily before crossing his arms and walking out of the drawing room to the stairs. He would have to go and explain this monstrous act to his waiting wife and doubted that either of them would be visited by sleep that night.

Chapter 16

The Cambray Theatre was full for the evening's performance. In the first circle and dress circle, the audience was mainly seated and the pit area at the front of the stage was packed with those jostling for standing room only. Watching from the luxury of a grand box were Mr and Mrs Mount, guests of Mr Hayne. The pair sat at the very edge of the space, their chairs side by side. Mr Mount rested his hands over the plush red velvet edge and both he and his wife searched the audience to see who was looking back up at them. Mr Hayne sat further into the enclosed space and had resigned himself to staring at the stage after a good attempt to make conversation with his future in-laws.

In the pit William Buckley glowered up at Joseph and the Mounts in the box. He stroked his chin and his lips curled up into a grim smile. 'I see things have moved on a pace.' He muttered to himself before turning and elbowing his friend Peters – a small stocky fellow. The pair were squeezed together in the crowded space. Buckley often preferred being in the pit to a box so he could look up and around unobserved.

'Do not look up but just listen.' Buckley bent sideways slightly and turned his face to his friend who grinned but kept his eyes ahead. 'Now, a Mr Hayne is sitting in the grand box. I want you to go up there and request that I speak with him here in the pit.'

'Now?' his friend looked about him and strained his neck to see out of the mass of people around and behind him.

'Yes, now man, it is important... I must see him before the play starts.' Buckley snapped and almost pushed his companion back out through the crowd and then looked up again at Joseph with narrowed eyes. He continued to stare, and a moment passed before he saw the young man getting out of his seat and retreating to the back of the box. Buckley was annoyed as he saw Joseph return to his seat and a few minutes later Peters returned, pushing his way through the disgruntled playgoers who surrounded him. As he reached Buckley, his face flushed. He caught his breath and shook his head.

'He refuses to come down, Buckley. He says he would be willing to speak to you outside the theatre during the first interval.' His friend now looked up at the box. Joseph was sitting back in his seat with his eyes on the stage. Mr and Mrs Mount were still leaning over the side and scanning the auditorium.

Buckley frowned. 'I see. Then that is what we will do.' His eyes were now focused on the stage as the lights dimmed and the orchestra struck up a lively tune. The grand stage curtains parted, and Buckley sighed and whispered to his friend, 'I am going for a drink. I will be back after the interval. Don't wait for me, my man.'

As he waded through the packed crowd, Buckley was elbowed and scowled at. On the stage, a man in a black tie was addressing the audience, promising 'an astounding evening with a one-act play prior to the main event and a comedic afterpiece.' Buckley scowled back as he heard whispers of, 'Is that Colonel Buckley? What is he doing in the pit?' He strode on and once out of the scrum, he headed up an aisle to the theatre bar. Joseph glanced over and saw his rival's movements. He quickly placed his hands in his lap, faced the stage again and pursed his lips.

The one-act play was short and as soon as the curtain came down, Joseph excused himself to his companions and walked out of the box and along a corridor to the entrance of the theatre. His hands clasped and unclasped beside him and his mind was racing. What does the blaggard want to see me about? he wondered. If he thinks he can challenge me about my betrothal, then he has met his match!

Once outside, Joseph turned and looked both ways.

'Mr Hayne.' Buckley was standing at the entrance to the back lane next to the theatre. He scowled and then turned, disappearing into the narrowness of the lane. Joseph followed nervously. As the young man turned the corner, he found Buckley standing in the middle of the lane. He had his arms crossed and he was frowning.

'I would rather not exchange pleasantries Mr Hayne. I would like an explanation of your conduct with respect to Miss Mount.' Buckley uncrossed his arms and took a step closer to Joseph. His height imposed on the young man who was forced to step back and look up into the older man's face.

Joseph almost laughed but instead spluttered, 'I...I don't feel that it would be honourable to disclose to you everything relative to my connection with Miss Mount.' He paused. 'But I can assure you, I have been informed by her father about some background. I understand you were engaged, but that this promise no longer stands.'

'I see.' Buckley rubbed his chin. 'You have heard this from her father? And did you ask Miss Mount about it? Did she not tell you of her engagement to me?

Joseph took another step back and looked down briefly before looking up again. He held his nose up in an attempt to meet Buckley's eyes on a level. 'Yes, she told me that you are no longer engaged. I made a proper and formal offer of marriage which was accepted by her father with his blessing.' Joseph now almost stood on tiptoes and puffed up his chest.

Buckley looked at him for a moment and then broke into an exaggerated laugh. His laugh became louder as he held his stomach and threw his head back. Joseph stood, stared at him and frowned. 'A blessing!' Buckley continued to laugh. 'My, my! I don't think you understand who and what you're dealing with here Mr Hayne.'

Joseph shook his head, 'Now look...'

'Now look, what?' Buckley suddenly snapped. He stopped laughing and took another step towards Joseph. 'Young fellow, her father told you she was engaged to me, and you have failed to do the decent thing and ask another gentleman about what belongs to him.'

Joseph stared at Buckley, his heart racing. 'The decent thing? If you had any... sense or... honour, you would have already married Miss Mount.' His voice stuttered slightly.

Buckley took another step closer to his rival. The pair were now standing less than a foot away from each other. 'Mr Hayne, I think you need to know the truth. You have been informed by Mr Mount of his daughter's engagement to me. But have you been informed that Miss Mount has borne two children? Two children who also belong to me?'

Joseph gasped and stifled a half shout, half scream. He stepped back and turned his body to face the wall, put his fist out and brought it hard against the surface. He stood, breathing raggedly for a few moments before turning slowly back to Buckley who sneered at him.

Joseph looked down at the ground and shook his head. 'Sir, I...I... did not know this information. How...? I do not believe it. How dare you sully her name with such falsehood. I can assure you she would have informed me of such a situation.'

Buckley continued to sneer, 'It appears you do not know her at all, Hayne. Have you not seen the silver locket around her neck which she grasps so tenderly. Who do you think is pictured inside that locket? I can tell you now it is our children.'

Joseph staggered backwards. 'Sir, I did not know this information. I see this is a difficult situation... I have walked into... but surely.' He lifted his head. 'What of *your* intention to marry Miss Mount?'

'I don't see that is any of your business, Hayne.' Buckley continued to stare down the young man. 'What has happened between Miss Mount and I is between us. Whatever she or her father has promised should be taken very lightly.' He smirked, 'She is an actress after all.'

Joseph stood with his mouth open. His fists clenched as he stared at Buckley in disbelief. 'How do I know you're not lying to me? You would say anything to…'

Before he could finish, Buckley lurched forward and grabbed the young man's collar with one strong hand and pulled his innocent face towards him. 'Lying to you!' he sneered. 'I wouldn't bother with a green like you.' Buckley spat the words into Joseph's terrified face. 'You don't know who you are dealing with here, young buck. I suggest you go back up to your box with the Mounts and enjoy your evening, if you can. Then, you'll end your association with Miss Mount and depart Cheltenham, if you know what's good for you.'

Buckley shook his victim with his strong arm and then spoke in a steadier but mocking tone, 'I will go and console Maria. You don't have to worry about that. You must realise that you are infatuated with a whore.' Buckley broke into a loud snorting laugh and before his rival could respond, he suddenly let go of Joseph's collar and with both hands pushed him hard, sending him crashing into the wall before he strode off down the lane and around the corner towards the theatre.

Joseph stood in the lane. He leaned against the wall, shaking his head slowly while pressing down his coat and smoothing his collar with trembling hands. He looked miserably about him and walked back down the passage in the footsteps of Buckley. For a moment, he stood outside the theatre door clenching and unclenching his fists. His heart was thundering and he frowned. 'Why has the devil not married her?' he exclaimed aloud. Looking up at the sky, he sighed. 'I will ask her why!' he exclaimed again as he rushed to the theatre door, grabbed it, and bounded in. As soon as he had reached the auditorium with the intention of dashing backstage, the bell sounded for the second act. Joseph stamped his foot. Do people know? He thought as theatre goers bustled past him to their seats.

Reluctantly returning to the box, he looked at his companions in disbelief and shock. Why did they not say? Is Buckley making this all up? His mind was spinning and as the curtain went up, he leaned over to see Buckley in the pit laughing with his friend. In the next moment, Maria entered the stage. Joseph stared at her beautiful face in disbelief. Why had she deceived him? At once he felt both wildly jealous and angry with the actress as he saw Buckley proudly looking on and whispering. Joseph was incensed and the second act seemed to drag on for a lifetime. Am I to forgive her for this too, he thought? Surely, I would be a fool to carry on pursuing her. Joseph had to confront her properly this time.

As soon as the curtain fell, Joseph bounded out of his seat, bowed to Mr and Mrs Mount, and charged backstage, not caring if Buckley would get there first.

Maria had barely entered her dressing room as Joseph was announced. She was sat at her dressing room table, the gas lights around the mirror creating a cosy glow in the red room. The actress looked at him expectantly, her faced flushed and her eyes wide.

'Oh, dear Joseph! You enjoyed the performance?' She loosened her corset slightly and beckoned him into the room.

Joseph held out his hands and moved slightly towards her before stopping awkwardly and rubbing his forehead with his hand. His face was red as he raised his voice, 'Miss Mount, it seems I have been grossly misled! Not only have I learned of the true nature of your engagement to Buckley, but he just now informed me, in a very rough manner, I might add, that you have borne him two children! Whatever I am to make of that?' Joseph's voice wobbled as it rose even higher.

Maria's eyes widened further as she stared at her suitor. There was a moment's silence as the pair stared at each other and then suddenly, Maria gave a loud sob and broke into tears. 'Oh Joseph, I have not been honourable. I have been trying to tell you.' Maria turned and scooped up her locket which was resting next to the mirror. She opened the treasure and then turned it to her suitor who stared in disbelief as he took it from her hands. Joseph stood looking at the portraits for a moment and then gave a small burst of laughter.

'Oh, I have been a fool! My friends warned me about women like you...'

Maria snatched the locket back, her face now fierce and frowning. 'Women like me!' she hissed. 'I see. Have you ever thought how some have not been honourable to me? How I long to be with my children; how I have been promised marriage and security time and time again?' She held back another sob. 'You begged me to marry you and, in truth Mr Hayne, I saw you as a way out. I saw your kindness and innocence and I thought... perhaps... one day my children could return to me and I could have the family I have always wanted.'

Joseph listened. His face had now slightly softened, and he nodded slowly before frowning. 'I have just been humiliated by Buckley. What a rogue! How have you let him destroy your life?' He held out his hands towards Maria.

'I make do Mr Hayne.' The actress looked towards the mirror and then down at her locket before sighing heavily. 'I miss my children dreadfully and I am fully aware of my foolish involvement with Colonel Buckley... My shame.' Maria put her hand to her heart and took a deep breath. 'It has been a weakness, but I do not intend to be weak again.' She turned towards the young man. 'Since I have met you, I now see what a man can offer: I feel safe with you; I feel like I can trust you.' She looked up at him with imploring eyes.

Tears had formed in Joseph's eyes which caused Maria to suddenly stand up and grasp his hands. He squeezed them in his and looked down at her.

'Oh Maria, I must say, I am quite moved by your sad story

and I admit… that my flame of love for you has not been quenched by the revelation. My love, my feelings remain unaltered, and I would like to still offer my hand in marriage. I just wish you had told me sooner.'

Maria's eyes widened. 'You still wish to… but what about my children?'

'I can offer security, but I am still a young man and would want an heir of my own. If your children are safely in the care of others, then surely they have grown used to their circumstances? What could we offer them here? If we marry, I will settle my fortune on you and if you should survive me, it will become your absolute property. But you must break all contact with that cad Buckley, and I will see to it that he receives exactly what he deserves. The arrogant…'

Maria shook her head and clutching the locket to her heart, she interrupted. 'Now that you know everything…can you not see a future with me and them? It would complete my life if they could come and live with us. Of course, I will break contact with Buckley, but my children…'

Joseph moved towards the actress, 'Dearest, yes, I know everything now… but you must let me think on it. In the meantime, let us fix a date for the wedding and may God strike me dead if ever I consent to separate myself from you.' He clutched her hands as Maria continued to sob softly as she put her head on his chest.

Maria nodded slowly, the locket still clutched tightly in her hand.

Chapter 17

There were many hazards in walking to Cheltenham's Market House, one being dodging the pitted troughs filled with horse excrement and mud. This inconvenience was eased slightly by the weekly flooding when waters from the River Chelt were diverted down the street by the owner of Barrett's Mill, with the purpose of cleaning the busy thoroughfare. Mr Arkell the miller often had to be reminded of his duties and was even fined if this task was not carried out periodically. Stepping-stones across the street afforded a more respectable way of getting to the other side, and Sarah the reverend's parlour maid gathered her skirts as she made her way to the market.

The Market House had a grand oriental-style arched entrance. People trundled in and out and once inside, the hustle and bustle of market life was overwhelming. Sarah edged past the stalls: a colourful abundance of fruits and vegetables, meat and fish, flowers and herbs were on display. Stall holders hawked their wares, and the grunts and smells of animals caused the maid to quicken her pace as she endeavoured to rush through her twice weekly duty of shopping for the cook. This morning, so soon after the horrific events at the reverend's home, she wanted to be back at Lansdown instead of being out and about amongst the voracious town gossips.

She examined the faces of those around her for any hint of knowing, listening hard for any talk of the scandal. She put her mind at rest as she realised that everyone was going about their business and quickly worked through the list of items requested by Harriet: onions, leeks, potatoes, two whole chickens and other sundries, and proceeded the way she had come through the arched entrance of the market.

Gathering her skirts for the stepping stones, Sarah was looking down as she bumped shoulders with Hetty who was walking hastily the other way. Maria's maid had been rushing from Bettison's Library further up the high street and had been looking down at the note she was carrying. The pair stood and looked at each other briefly in shock before Hetty quickly placed her hand on Sarah's shoulder.

'Oh, my... I'm so sorry, I wasn't looking.'

Sarah looked down at her basket still safely laden with her wares. She briefly glanced at Hetty's note before smiling, 'I wasn't looking either. Hetty, isn't it? From the orphanage?' Sarah stood back and took her fellow maid in with a glance up and down.

'Sarah, is it you? Yes, it's Hetty... oh goodness, how long has it been since we were there? You were a few years above me? I thought it was you when I was with my mistress in that lovely sweet shop.'

'Gosh, yes.' Sarah smiled. 'It seems like a long time ago now when we were at the orphanage.'

'Five years ago now for me. Did you go straight into service for the reverend?'

Sarah nodded as she took Hetty's arm and guided her companion to the side of the street to talk. Two ladies had stopped to look at the maids and whisper behind gloves. It was clear that there was a different class of Cheltonian on the high street; ones who were up to date with the very latest gossip. Sarah looked at her fellow maid and saw that Hetty had noticed the whisperers too. She grimaced in response and Sarah grasped her arm firmer and led her back into the bustle of the Market House.

Once back in the safety of the busy market, Sarah stood

close to her companion so that she might whisper. 'Hetty, you must have heard?' Maria's maid was not used to the sounds and smells of the market as she was never tasked with the duty of shopping. She looked about her for a moment, then drew closer to her old friend.

'Heard about Miss Mount and Mr Hayne?' She looked quizzically at Sarah.

Sarah stared at her. 'No, about the Reverend Cole and his... delivery?'

'His delivery? No.' Hetty hesitated. 'I thought you wanted to ask me about Miss Mount?'

'Oh Hetty, no. Haven't you heard about the poor baby? Delivered to the reverend in a basket. It was dead... I was there... it was awful Hetty. I haven't spoken to anyone about it since, but I keep dreaming about the poor little thing.' Sarah suddenly burst into tears.

Maria's maid stood in shock for a moment and then placed her hand gently on Sarah's arm. Sarah continued to cry. Hetty whispered, 'My goodness, who on earth would do something like that? Or why?'

Sarah looked down; she wiped her face with the back of her hand and looked back up at her old friend, 'Nobody knows. The poor thing was taken to the workhouse the next morning by the constable, there's to be an investigation... I ain't had chance to talk to nobody.' Sarah's loud sobs resumed, alerting a nearby stallholder who looked briefly across but quickly went back to his business.

Hetty moved closer to Sarah and held her shoulders gently. 'My dear, what an awful thing. Who else was there? Is the family supporting you?'

'Yes,' Sarah's tears still streamed but she was soothed by Hetty's kind words. 'They are always so supportive, but the reverend... he's a changed man... he's barely come out of his study at all and everyone must be talking about it. Or if not now, then soon. There was a note tied to the babe's finger which said, "Behold Thy Likeness." If that comes out in the investigation, then surely everyone will wonder if the child was his?'

Hetty looked at the maid with wide eyes. 'Do *you* think it was his?'

'No, I don't think so.' Sarah answered. 'But I think some people want to destroy the reverend and will stoop to this awful level... you won't tell anyone, will you Hetty? I don't mean to be a gossip, I just needed to tell someone...' The maid suddenly noticed the rolled paper still clutched tightly in Hetty's hand. 'What is that?'

Hetty unrolled the paper slowly and turned it round. 'Oh Sarah, I too have been witness to scandal. I suppose you haven't heard about Miss Mount's drama either?'

Sarah was looking at the picture on the paper. It was a crude tracing of a caricature showing three figures standing centrally in a room. A lady stood in the middle of two men. Scribbled on the bottom of the picture were the words, 'The Double Dealers: two strings to your bow or who's the dupe? A melodrama to be performed at The Cambray Theatre.' Looking through the door into the room was a maid and a little girl and in a speech bubble was written, 'Stop my dear, I don't know which of the papa's you will have yet.'

Sarah stared at the picture, 'No, I haven't heard of this. What is it?'

Hetty sighed, 'It's my drawing of a magazine caricature. I have just been to the library to see it. My mistress wanted to know what it said.'

'But what is it about? We have been so caught up in everything at Lansdown.'

'Oh Sarah, it seems we are both caught up in scandal. But I will not burden you with my gossip now. I imagine everyone will be talking about it today. Now, you must stay strong. I must be getting back as I am sure you will be. I hope we meet again in happier circumstances.'

The maids glanced round the market before leaving through the arched entrance arm in arm. Once on the high street, they embraced quickly before going their separate ways back to the drama of their individual households.

Chapter 18

The reverend had been unusually absent from the breakfast room at Lansdown House that morning. The usual routine was for Sarah to serve him tea and bread at 6.30am sharp before he left at 7am on his fifteen-minute walk down the sloping Bayshill Estate to St. Mary's Church.

It was no usual morning as the day of the Cheltenham Races had arrived. It was also the Buns and Tea event and every citizen of the town and beyond would be out enjoying revelries of one kind or another. All of the children from the various National and Sunday church schools had been invited to join the clergy at tables placed along the tree-lined path on the Well Walk. The catering had been arranged and a band was set to play. As with other years, it was expected to be a crowded and joyful event with onlookers marvelling at the reverend's influence for wholesome good in the town.

Instead, the reverend could be found sitting on a bench in his garden. A beautiful morning mist created an ethereal haze of light across the walled space. An apple tree cast a shadow across a meadow area with a gravel walkway running from the bench, beneath a stone arch, and through to the driveway. The reverend stared at a pond near the bench. He called it his 'wilderness' - a mixture of large leafy plants and tall spiky grasses which grew in scattered fashion around the small dark pool. Moss covered stones, logs and gnarly roots nestled on the sides and little newts poked their heads up before sinking back into the depths.

Elizabeth looked out of an upstairs window of the house and saw her husband seated. He was wearing his black robes, held a bible in both hands and was staring intently at the pond. She threw on her tea-gown – a soft flowing robe of fine cream silk –and hurried downstairs with her brown curls loose about her shoulders. She opened the back door, gathered the robe at the foot and stepped along the gravel walkway. Elizabeth worked hard to project a positive energy and cheerful smile, but inside her mind and emotions were in turmoil. She came to a halt in front of the reverend, noting the red rims of his eyes and the heavy bags beneath them as he looked up at her. He held her gaze for a moment before looking down again at the pond.

Elizabeth forced a bright tone, 'Dear, have you had breakfast? We must be off soon.'

The reverend sighed and looked again at his wife. 'Yes, we must. We must, my dear.' But still he only shook his head, looked down at the pond and sighed again.

'Oh, my love.' Elizabeth sat beside him and put her hand on his knee. 'Yes, we must. As we always have done. We must not let this evil deed stop us. Yours is a Godly cause and most people in this town know you for all your good works.'

The reverend shook his head again, placing his hand in hers. His other hand maintained a tight grip on his bible. 'Elizabeth, dear, I have indeed encountered a number of challenges over the years and weathered them all, but this... this act. I do not know who or why such a... how can I serve all these children today? How can I meet their faithful parents and face them on this day?'

Elizabeth paused and squeezed his hand, 'We have done all we can do. The poor child is now being buried and it is out of our hands. The inquest is forthcoming, and we can't dwell on who committed this awful crime or who the unfortunate child belonged to. We have no control over it. What we do have control over is how we continue with our duties: how we always do our duty. How you, my love, despite all the challenges and all those who seek to derail you, carry on. That is what I most admire about you. Do not let this abhorrent act steer you off your course.' Elizabeth gently laid a hand on the reverend's cheek and turned his face to look into his eyes which were welling up with tears.

'Oh Elizabeth, this is why I love you so! Your practicality, your devotion to me and my cause.' He now placed his bible on the bench and held both of her hands in his. 'I do not usually concern myself with what people say and what they think about my preaching and my causes, but this...surely... this is already a scandal which everyone will be talking about... and even asking me about today. Surely, people will say that the infant is linked to me... that it is even mine! Do you believe me that it isn't? That this is an evil to try and stop me in my tracks?' he looked pleadingly at her.

Elizabeth clasped his hands even tighter, 'Of course I believe you. I believe in *you*. Husband, I have been reading the papers carefully, and be assured that there is another scandal being talked about in this town which is sure to fulfil the public's satisfaction for gossip for a long time.'

The reverend frowned as Elizabeth continued, 'Yes, there has been a report of the incident relating to our delivery, but it has been written as a notice of inquest. There is so much going on in Cheltenham this season. But... we must have faith in the good Lord and not be diverted from our cause. Now Francis, we have only half an hour before the clergy arrive for our special day. The children will then be arriving and we must be ready.'

*

On the Well Walk the clergy had gathered. The towering elm trees swayed in the gentle mid-morning breeze and visitors to the spas promenaded the shaded gravel walk. Meanwhile, those heading to the races entered Cheltenham from all directions to gather on the high street, drawn by the sound of lively fiddlers. Handsome carriages swooped down from the Montpellier Promenade and horsemen cantered by. Those on foot were mainly in groups: men calling loudly, women behind them, already in a merry state. Those off to the races preferred ale to tea, but a few stopped to observe the scene being prepared by the clergy. The tall tapering steeple of the parish church rose in the centre of the Well Walk in the distance and overlooked the bustling scene.

Tables and chairs had been carried from the church hall and placed all along the walk and covered with tablecloths so that the Buns and Tea event could be held in full view. Plates were piled high with an assortment of breads, rolls, cakes, cookies, and sweet treats. The tables groaned beneath the weight of cakes with butter icing, sandwiches with potted paste, and scones with jam. A lively band played as the reverend and Elizabeth hurried down the walk. Tables were already filling up with excitable children: the youngsters from ages five to ten had been reminded to sit politely at the table with their hands underneath them until the reverend had spoken. Their eyes were wide as they stared at the abundance in front of them and as the reverend approached there was a clatter and a resounding cheer from the tables.

Following closely behind Elizabeth and the reverend were Mr Bonfils and his staff. All were dressed in pristine white coats and held a multitude of yellow jellies aloft on silver trays. Another great cheer rose, and all eyes were on the trays of wobbling sculptures; the children had never seen anything like it before and a hush descended on the tables where the jellies were placed. Parents and the town's clergy looked on in delight.

Now, near the head of the tables, Elizabeth beamed at the scene and turned to her husband. 'You see how many people have turned out for this? This was your idea and your creation. Everyone knows of your good works in the town, and it is only the few who try to bring you down for their own ends. Now, I think you had better give your speech and instructions to start.'

The reverend nodded, and smiling to those near, he signalled to a robed man standing at the side of the tables and a bell was rung. The clergy and the parents put fingers to their lips and the reverend walked a few steps to the head of the top table, ready to speak. The chatter gradually stopped, and he bowed to the many expectant faces looking up at him. Elizabeth stood by his side as he paused for a moment to survey the scene before him.

He cleared his throat, 'My brethren... children...' He paused again as his voice broke. He took out a large handkerchief from his robe pocket and wiped his eyes. 'It is my pleasure to host you once again at our annual Buns and Tea party.' The reverend looked at Elizabeth who smiled encouragingly. 'I am grateful for your attendance here.' He bowed again and smiled at the parents who had gathered nearby. 'Now, I won't keep you from this feast before you, but may I thank you and let us pray.' The reverend bowed his head, put his hands together and the children and all those standing followed. 'May the grace of our Lord Jesus Christ, and the love of God, and the fellowship of the Holy Spirit be with us all, now and evermore. Amen.' The reverend nodded and the bell rang again. The children gave a cheer and for the next few precious moments all were occupied in the choosing of treats and tasting of buns.

The reverend walked up and down the tables and smiled. His injured faith and heart were softened by the scene momentarily, but then he suddenly froze. His expression changed to horror as he turned to face the side of the Well Walk where, just metres away and followed by an entourage of three mounted men, Colonel Buckley was trotting his horse slowly past the bystanders. The reverend would not have seen him over the heads of the crowd if he had not been on his horse and as the reverend stared, some of the children looked up at his startled face. Buckley suddenly stopped, surveyed the scene in front of him and then met the reverend's gaze. His powerful, glossy chestnut horse tossed its mane and snorted. Buckley was wearing his yellow tweed hunt jacket with green collar over a white shirt and his black leather breeches clung to his sturdy legs. His face was fixed into a stern glare. The two men stared at each other. Their faces suddenly frozen in cold-blooded calm, but concealing boiling anger under the surface. The moment stood still and the reverend continued to fix his gaze on the horseman. But then Buckley smirked, pushed back his hat, jolted his horse away and cantered smoothly towards the high street.

The reverend shook his head and reached for the back of one of the children's chairs near him. Some of the onlookers had turned to witness the encounter and whispered to each other. Elizabeth had noticed and moved closer, reaching her hand to her husband's arm. He shook his head again and then advanced towards a steward, relieved him of a teapot and began to dispense tea into the tin mugs of the children. His hands still shaking from the encounter, the reverend forced a smile at the little faces looking up at him. Elizabeth wasted no time in joining him and picked up a teapot to walk up and down the tables in service.

Among the crowds at the side of the Well Walk, Lord and Lady Croft were standing with Lady Glenfield and had witnessed the whole encounter. They had paused their carriages on the way to the races and stepped out to view the charitable scene. Standing on the gravel walk, wearing a rich burgundy pelisse robe with matching bonnet – its brim widened into a large halo about her face– Lady Croft announced loudly to anyone near, 'This season is proving to be the busiest yet, what with all the scandal.'

Lady Glenfield, wearing an equally grand day dress of pale blue silk with matching bonnet attached with fluttering blue ribbon, grimaced at her companion and moved a step away.

Unperturbed, Lady Croft stepped towards her, the sausage curls arranged at her temples jiggled as she shook her head with excitement. 'Oh, I would not choose to be anywhere else in all the land. Oh, come, are you not intrigued by it all, Lady Glenfield? Not only do we have the town's dogmatic reverend tested on this most vital of weeks, but we have a love triangle to entertain us.'

Lord Croft stepped quickly away with his betting book. Lady Glenfield remained where she was, hesitated and then answered coolly, 'Lady Croft, I would have thought someone of your breeding would show a little more decorum and sympathy to those involved.'

Lady Croft looked around to see her husband still studiously absorbed in his book. She opened and closed her mouth as she turned back to Lady Glenfield, her voice louder. 'Well, my dear, this is the first time you have showed sympathy to those caught up in the town's scandals, I must say.'

Lady Glenfield looked straight ahead at the scene: the reverend and Elizabeth were serving a group of children. Despite their clear undernourishment and ragged clothes, the children's faces were innocent and merry. She turned back to her companion and spoke sternly, 'Whoever committed the awful crime against the reverend should be punished. Whatever we think of our incumbent, we must admire his cause and the fact he is still here today at this event. So many others of our standing now support him.' She waved her arm to encompass the scene.

Lady Croft stood in silence for a moment. Flustered, she then nodded quickly, her sausage curls flounced. 'Well enough of him, what of Miss Mount, Buckley, and Mr Hayne? I hear the marriage has been confirmed – there was a notice in the *Cheltenham Chronicle*. Does the young gentleman know about

Buckley, I wonder? Does he know of their children? I can't see Buckley allowing it.'

Lady Glenfield took a deep breath and turned to her companion. 'Once again Lady Croft, I see we are at opposite ends of a spectrum. Maria Mount has been through enough without further interference from Colonel William Buckley. That cad has got away with far too much for far too long. Probably because of the likes of you supporting him and his ways. Have you not heard that he has even been associated with the awful incident involving the reverend?' she asked sharply.

Lady Croft spluttered and took a step back. 'The reverend seems perfectly fine from where I am standing. And yes, I have heard that William has been accused of the crime and I totally dispute it. He would never do such a thing.' Her voice was now high which caused some of those near to turn and look.

Lady Glenfield simply nodded, 'Perhaps it is time finally for good to prevail in this town, and I for one am in full support of that. Good day, Lady Croft.' The lady walked off to her carriage without a backwards glance, leaving Lady Croft once again opening and closing her mouth. Lord Croft was still writing in his betting book.

'Did you hear that husband? How Lady Glenfield just spoke to me?'

Lord Croft raised an eyebrow, 'Yes, I heard her. How very rude!' he then turned away with a small smirk.

Chapter 19

By noon the high street was the scene of the usual Cheltenham Race Day bustling: sporting gentlemen and members of the turf clubs congregated around the entrance to The Plough Inn and Assembly Rooms, speculating on the state of the ground and registering in their betting books their hopes and fears of 'the favourite.' Booth men and publicans elbowed them at every turn, and boys with unwashed faces and unclean hands bawled out regularly: 'Correct lists of the horses gentlemen, names, weights, and colours of the riders.' Adding to the noise and chaos of the scene were post chaises from the country, flys from nearer by, and anonymous horsemen from nobody knew where.

In one of the fly carriages sat Joseph, dressed for his first race meeting in a dark green tweed coat with matching breeches. He clutched a betting booklet in his hand and was listening avidly to his companion opposite, fellow Cheltenham speculator Thomas Jameson: a lively man who liked to talk about his investments in the town as much as his chances at the races. As the carriage left the high street en route to the racecourse at Prestbury Park, Jameson - a regular of the Cheltenham Races - was in full flow as he sat forward in his seat.

'The Duke of Gloucester attends every meeting and is still among those subscribing 100 guineas.' Joseph nodded at his companion's remarks as the carriage followed others on its short and steady climb out of town. The races were not really of much interest to Joseph, and he certainly did not want to encounter Colonel Buckley. But a newcomer must experience this great spectacle, he thought. Soon, the gravel paths gave way to rough tracks, and instead of grand white buildings and villas, fields stretched out before them, interrupted only by the occasional allotment or cottage alongside the track.

Jameson removed a silver flask from the breast of his jacket and took a gulp before extending it to his companion. 'Port?'

Joseph blushed but then smiled and took the flask. Taking a swig, he then turned his face to the window to disguise a wince. He was not a drinking man but believed if he was to enter into the spirit of the Cheltenham Races, he should go along with tradition.

Alongside the carriage walked racegoers, some in smart dresses and tailcoats and others in near rags, many drinking from bottles while others stopped at make-shift stalls selling beer, gin, snuff, and even parasols. The parasol seller was already doing a brisk business as a cloudless sky promised a sunny and warm day, with little shade to be had at the racecourse.

'You know the races used to be up on the hills?' Jameson asked, ducking down in his seat and pointing to Cleeve Hill in the distance. Joseph bent forward to look himself.

'Crowds flocked to it.' Jameson explained. 'Oh it was the greatest attraction of the year and rather chaotic if you ask me. The path up the hill was always strewn with sideshows and gambling booths and the place was rife with pickpockets. The only place you were really safe was in the grandstand, and you know what happened to that?'

Joseph shook his head, his eyes wide. He had now slipped his gold watch on a chain attached to his waistcoat into his breast pocket. 'No... I don't know what happened. I do hope it's a bit more organised this year.' He laughed nervously.

Jameson took another swig from his flask, and then offered it again to Joseph who reluctantly accepted. 'It burned down.

Everyone saw it from the Promenade. Seven years ago now, on one of the nights after the races. They say that the Cheltenham Reverend Cole's lot had something to do with it. Never proven of course, but there was such strong feeling and even protests up at the course that day. I was there: it was chaos. Since then, the races have been out of town. I never thought I would see the day of their return. But here we are.' Jameson sat forward again excitedly.

Joseph was nodding, still wide-eyed, 'My goodness. And what finally brought the races back to Cheltenham?'

'Money, Hayne! And tradition.' Jameson laughed. 'All the old families are still very much in support of the races so it will take a formidable effort to remove these traditions completely. Although, that darned reverend has had a good crack at it so far.'

After a final steep incline up the track and into a wider open gravelled area, the carriage finally brought the pair to their destination: the entrance to the racecourse. Wooden gates had been installed with two narrow entrances: one for the masses and the other for those of rank and respectability. Jameson jumped out of the carriage and Joseph followed him closely through the crowds.

'We will quickly be away from the rabble Hayne. The races really do attract some quite unwelcome elements: make sure you keep your wits about you!'

Once through the entrance, Jameson turned to the left where the new grandstand stood. The long wooden building had tiered seating at the front and was painted white. There were staircases on either side which led to a reception room above which extended the length and breadth of the building. From there, the higher-class spectator was invited to socialise and watch the races from its large arched windows on the balcony. While he was jostled along by the crowd, Joseph could see well-dressed people of rank gathering and looking out over the course and checking the betting booklets.

Jameson led Joseph to the steep steps at the side of the grandstand and soon they were out of the hordes. Upon entering the top tier, Joseph immediately spotted Buckley standing with a group of men. Joseph stared. Buckley was in the centre of the group holding court. Some were raising glasses and a flamboyantly dressed man in red tweed slapped him on the back and laughed loudly. Buckley suddenly glanced over and saw his rival. Joseph felt a surge of anger but quickly looked away. The shade inside the grandstand was welcome, but with no wind, he began to feel hot. Buckley's voice boomed louder at his audience. Jameson pointed, 'You know Colonel Buckley and Fulwar Chamberlayne of course. They are with the Irish Colonel Charretie and his men. All patrons of the races and very important you know? And look there is his brother Craven Buckley standing over there.' Jameson nodded at the MP who stood with another man in a corner and then made his way to the bar.

Joseph glanced back and narrowed his eyes at Buckley and then moved over to the side of the grandstand balcony to look out at the racecourse. Crowds gathered at the one-bar fences near to the starting line. Many were huddled in groups and others took refuge in the comfort of their carriages. Joseph saw a tall, thin man who was standing at the side of the track and pointing to the paddock. He looked over to where he signalled and at that moment, a bell sounded. Twelve horses were walked out by grooms and a silence descended on the crowd. In the stillness, there was a whinnying as the colourful, silk-clad jockeys walked beside their mounts carrying saddles. As the horses reached the front of the grandstand, their nostrils already flaring, the jockeys talked briefly to their trainers who were standing around, swung the saddles up, fixed them onto the great beasts and then swung themselves onto the horse's backs. They cantered a little, controlling the brown and lean animals with expert skill, circled, and then positioned themselves at the start. Joseph looked over again at Buckley who was now standing at the side of the balcony, his face fixed in anticipation of the first race.

Jameson returned from the bar with two drinks, and, at the same time, a waiter arrived in front of Joseph. On his tray were two glasses holding dark liquid. 'Compliments of the race organisers, Sirs.' The waiter bowed as Jameson laughed, put his drinks down on a table and scooped both glasses up, offering one to Hayne and downing his own in one. Joseph hesitated briefly and held his glass, stared at Jameson and copied the action with a splutter and then a slight cough. He grinned.

Suddenly, there was a huge cheer among the crowd as the first race started and everyone's eyes were drawn to the course. The sound of thundering hooves carried into the grandstand as clods of earth were thrown up into the air. The horses galloped along at a tremendous pace and as they turned the far corner, the noise in the crowd rose. Joseph stood transfixed as he watched them disappear into the distance towards Prestbury Manor. Another lap and another drink was handed to him. As horses and riders entered into the third and final lap, the screams and cheers from the crowd reached a deafening peak. As the horses crossed the finish line, winners jumped up and congratulated, while losers angrily tore up tickets. Joseph watched in amazement as the crowds dispersed until the next race and reassembled at the betting posts which were dotted all along the course. As there was a gambling booth in the grandstand reception room, Joseph steadied himself, opened his betting book and followed his companion in putting on his first bet.

'Mayfly – first rate character it says?' The young man looked up from his betting book to Jameson who was studying his own book.

'Ah yes, Colonel Buckley's horse. Always winning that one.'

Joseph glanced down again and frowned. He picked another horse and placed some notes into the boothman's hands. Jameson's eyes widened. 'Are you sure, that much? For your first horse?'

'Yes, I'm sure.' Joseph nodded. The drink had made him bold. If his horse won over Buckley's, he would make sure to celebrate his win for all to hear.

When all eyes were on the racecourse again, Joseph stared out at the horses at the starting line. The great beasts were already glistening in the heat. He picked his out as the jockeys jostled for position and when they had assembled in a haphazard line, there was a sudden shout. The horses took off with a hop, gaining pace as they galloped closer and closer to the grandstand.

'And they're off!' Jameson shouted, punching the air amid the growing roar of the crowd. A jolt of excitement seared through Joseph's body. After his jockey seemed to take the first lengths at an easy pace, on the second turn he saw him urging the animal on. The charging horses raced around the bend, their nostrils flaring. Joseph could see the steam rising off their hinds and the jockeys' grimacing faces as they drew their elbows in tighter and whipped harder and harder. Joseph stole a look at Buckley who was leaning out over the balcony shouting for Mayfly, his loud companions joining in with the roar.

The shouts and screams of the crowd intensified as the charging runners started on the last lap. Joseph's horse was third as it rounded the bend towards them and galloped up the straight towards the finish line. Now the whole of the grandstand crowd was on its feet, shouting and calling out and the roar of the racegoers grew until it reached a crescendo. Joseph joined in and hollered at the top of his voice, his arm in the air, fist clenched. He fixed his eyes on his horse as it ran past, thrusting its muzzle forward and drumming the ground with its hooves as it surged towards the final line. His horse inching past Mayfly with its yellow-silked jockey. The horses were going neck and neck and then Joseph's bounded into second place then a final push... Joseph punched the air and roared with delight as his horse crossed the line in first place.

Jameson nearly jumped on his companion and hugged him tightly. The two men jumped up and down clumsily. There was a cheer from those near and men slapped and patted him on the back with glee.

'Drinks for everyone in the room!' Joseph shouted.

Mayfly had come in third. Its owner glared at Joseph from across the room, his face furious. Joseph glared back and turned to the group of men who had gathered to toast his race success. His voice was loud and slurred as he raised his glass. 'A toast to my winning horse and my beautiful wife to be!' Those nearby cheered and Jameson clinked his glass against his friend's, pouring more port into it. Buckley strode across the room, knocking a chair out of the way and descending the stairs.

The excitement settled as people gathered at the booth, and Jameson glanced over at the departing Buckley before turning back to Joseph. 'Your betrothed Miss Mount, is she not in attendance today?'

Joseph slurred. 'Oh no, she is enjoying a day of rest. Quite punishing, all those performances you know. She really is quite a talent. I am a very lucky man.' He smiled like a giddy schoolboy.

'So you are Mr Hayne.' Jameson slapped him on the back and poured him another drink.

'Another toast to Miss Mount, I mean Mrs Hayne!' he laughed.

As the sport continued late into the afternoon, the rising temperature drove the mass of crowds to seek shade anywhere possible, from makeshift tents made out of shawls and other garments to the underside of carriages and carts at the sides of the course. As the final race started, the drunken racegoers surged again towards the fences. Many of the gamblers now leaned on the rails with unkempt hair and fevered eyes. The heat and the noise were intense as the horses sped towards the final line with Jameson's horse coming in first. Joseph

133

joined him again in punching the air and enveloped him in a crushing hug. Joseph stumbled and Jameson clumsily righted him as they laughed.

As soon as the last race was over, the majority of the crowd quickly dispersed. Some men hung about the betting booths and those in the grandstand slowly made their way down the stairs. Buckley and his men were nowhere to be seen as Jameson and Joseph stumbled down the steep steps, clutching at the handrails. Joseph laughed as he nearly tripped at the bottom, his companion catching him before he fell flat on his face. The pair were caught up in a throng of merry people all moving to the exit. At first they were together, Hayne holding his winning ticket aloft and pointing to Jameson. Then, suddenly, the men were separated as a pushing increased from behind. Joseph saw the exit and turned around to gesture to his friend but was suddenly knocked hard from behind and found himself being half-carried and half-pushed through the crowd. He cried out in terror and tried to free his arms and turn his head but was overpowered and bundled into a waiting carriage. A single feeble cry sounded as the door was slammed closed, and with a flick of the reins, the carriage was gone.

Chapter 20

Tired from her performance the evening before and uninterested in the hustle and bustle of the races, Maria was spending her Sunday enjoying a late-morning promenade with her entourage.

Her heart was full and her chatter was easy and light as her group made their way along the Montpellier Promenade to The Jar and Pineapple. Sunlight filtered through the windows onto the pastel walls which seemed to glow, while the long copper counter glinted its welcome. As usual, Mr Bonfils was behind the counter wearing his wide, welcoming smile. He gestured to a seat in the corner and Maria and her two companions; Bess and Jerome, settled into the space while others in the shop looked on with awe at the group. Maria wore a striking bright blue gown and held a pretty blue reticule, while Bess showed off her impressive bosom with a low-cut gown in the brightest yellow. Jerome wore a flamboyant jacket and matching breeches in pale pink. His frilly white shirt was open at the front to reveal the top of his chest. All spoke in loud, theatrical voices, oblivious to the stares.

Mr Bonfils swept over to greet them. 'Miss Mount, it is always a pleasure to host you here at The Jar and Pineapple.' He bowed as she nodded and smiled. 'And your friends? Have you visited before?' Mr Bonfils' gaze rested on Jerome's broad open face and his eyes wandered briefly to the man's exposed chest. Jerome smiled knowingly in response and stretched his pink arm out to shake the confectioner's hand. 'Jerome D'Sule, a pleasure!'

'Arnaud Bonfils.' he bowed. Their handshake lingered longer than others.

Maria stared, 'Arnaud, well we have got his name out of him.' She laughed and winked at her friends. 'This is Bess Boothy, and neither she nor Jerome have visited before. I've been telling everyone at the theatre to visit you, Mr Bonfils.'

The confectioner bowed again and gestured the group to a table in the corner. 'Ah, Madame, I am always most grateful. And what is your wish today? I have just made a delightful new creation with my ices; would you like to try? See if you can guess the flavour?'

Maria laughed and clapped her hands together as they were led to their seats. 'Oh, Mr Bonfils, another new creation? Of course, let us all try it.' She opened her hands to her friends as the confectioner bowed again and hurried off to the kitchen. Bess giggled and Jerome licked his lips as they settled at the table and looked around.

'A regular here then Maria?' he laughed.

'Oh yes, it's a favourite place and you are in for a treat. Did you know that the ice for the ice creams comes from a deep store in the Montpellier Gardens over there?'

As the group looked out of the window, the shop door opened. A boy wearing a jacket worn at the elbows stood on the doorstep, his eyes downcast. He looked over at Maria and then started to approach. A waiter quickly intercepted him. A few words were spoken, and the boy stood still while the waiter walked over to Maria's table and nodded over to the youngster.

'Madam, this boy is urgently requesting that you take a note he has been instructed to deliver to you.'

Maria looked at her friends with her eyebrows raised, and then turned back to the waiter, 'Oh, of course.' Maria laughed and then nodded to the boy who approached with the note in his hand. He bowed nervously and Maria stared.

'What is this do you think?' Maria turned to her friends.

'Another fan note no doubt?' Jerome laughed, gazing on.

'Who has sent you?' Maria smiled at the boy who shook his head and shrugged. She took the letter and gave the boy a coin before he quickly turned and scurried from the shop. She then looked down at the note; it was a cream envelope with a red seal and addressed to Miss M. Mount in a hand she did not recognise. She carefully opened it, looking up at her friends and smiling. Others in the room had briefly stopped talking and were staring at her but as she looked around, they glanced away. Maria frowned slightly and then opened the envelope. As she read it, her face dropped but then she quickly composed herself and stuffed the letter back into its envelope.

Bess and Jerome stared at their friend. 'Is all well, my dear?' Bess asked. Maria tore her gaze from the envelope to look up, her lips pressed together as she answered slowly.

'It is from... Mr Hayne.' She paused and then whispered, 'He is... he is... calling off the marriage.' She pushed the letter over to Jerome who opened it quickly and scanned the page.

'I regret to inform you...' Jerome read. 'Regret to inform... what sort of message is this? That our betrothal is off? Does he not say why?' he passed it to Bess who read the text and then frowned.

'Surely, he would explain in person, no? And how did the messenger know you were here? Why not leave it at your home?' Bess had now raised her voice. People in the room were watching and Maria leaned forward to her friends.

'I do not know.' Maria whispered. She sighed and gulped back a tear. Mr Bonfils had come out from the kitchen and had observed the messenger's departure, along with Maria and her friend's reactions in his wake. He bustled over to her table, not failing to notice the curious whispers of his other customers.

'Miss Mount? Can I help? Can I get you anything?'

Maria waved her hand and quickly put the note into her reticule. 'Everything is fine Mr Bonfils. Please, bring out your creation.' The confectioner stood and stared for a moment before he bowed and bustled off again.

Maria turned to her friends. 'Let us stay. I will not allow this to ruin our day. How many times have I been let down by men?' she sighed. Her friends were silent for a moment as she wiped away a tear. 'No, you must not be concerned. This is the life of an actress. I can cope with another drama.' Maria laughed and looked around the room. Some were still stealing looks at the actress to see her reaction to the drama. Maria smiled steadily at them and then turned to her friends again. 'I will not think of this now.'

'But...' Bess protested.

'No.' Maria said firmly. 'I will deal with it later.' She looked steadily at her friends, forcing her lips up into a smile.

'Forget about him.' Bess whispered suddenly. 'This is the life of an actress. You cannot expect a man like Hayne to believe he is lucky enough to have secured you.'

Maria stared at her friend who continued, 'Our reputation, my dear Maria... you cannot expect to live like everyone else. Jerome, aren't I right?' The actor shrugged but looked sympathetically at Maria who still looked crestfallen. Bess tried to pacify after her strong words. 'Well, I for one like this life. No one to do bidding to: I do exactly as I wish.' She gave a cackling laugh which made Jerome and then Maria follow in mirth. The other customers looked on in fascination.

All eyes in the room then followed Mr Bonfils who stepped out of the backroom with his best creation yet: a sculpted ice in the shape of a pineapple. Arriving slowly at Maria's table, it was no bigger than her hand. The bright yellow ice resembled the exotic fruit to perfection. Its spiky sides had been expertly sculpted and the confectioner had even topped his creation with sculpted leaves. The whole room of customers stared at the pineapple in delight. Bess clapped her hands and Jerome opened his mouth in surprise.

'Oh Mr Bonfils, you are a genius!' Maria cried. 'It seems

such a shame to eat it!' The treat was placed in the centre of the table and the three stared at the pineapple for a while before carefully picking up their spoons and scooping them into the ice cream. The mixture melted in their mouths and the confectioner clapped his hands. The whole experience lifted the spirits.

'Enjoy!' Mr Bonfils beamed as he moved to depart.

Maria looked up at him, 'Oh this is truly outstanding Mr Bonfils! Are you married? If you are, then your wife must feel very lucky.'

'Married to my art only.' He gave his well-practised response, glanced at Jerome and laughed.

As the confectioner turned, the door suddenly opened again and in burst Joseph. The customers were astounded; their mouths open and spoons held in mid-air as the young gentleman stood in the doorway much like the messenger boy who had been there before him. His coat was ripped and his hair matted. His eyes looked drawn, he had lost the blush on his cheeks and his face was dirty.

Maria suddenly paused in her sampling of the pineapple and looked him up and down, stood up quickly and rushed towards her suitor. 'We must not talk here. Let us promenade to a quieter place. My friends will follow, and you can explain all there.'

She was almost motherly in her direction as she led him by the arm back to the open door. Maria seemed to have complete control of the situation as she pushed Joseph gently out into the street and turned to address the now silent customers and Mr Bonfils. 'Mr Bonfils, Ladies and Gentlemen, I must apologise for this most dramatic interruption. Now please, enjoy your afternoon.' She walked out with her friends following, at first reluctantly and with glances over their shoulders at the abandoned ice cream and Mr Bonfils, but they then followed quickly behind her.

Once out on the promenade, there were less stares than

in the shop but the sight of the famous actress with a wild looking young man was enough to make most people stop with mouths open and titter behind gloves. Maria held Joseph's elbow and quickly guided him across the promenade to the shade of the trees edging Montpellier Gardens. She then led him alongside the Montpellier Spa Buildings – a long line of newly built terraced town houses.

'My... d...dear...' Joseph began to stutter as he stumbled along. Maria still guided him by the arm.

'Do not talk until we are on the Broad Walk.' Maria hissed at her companion. The pair swiftly covered ground and reached the end of the buildings where there were no longer any promenaders. Bess and Jerome still followed behind as they turned left and then left again, hurrying back along the Broad Walk towards the little frequented Sherborne Spa. As they reached the building, set in gardens with high trees, they saw a distant couple in the grounds. The spa was a smaller version of the Montpellier Spa with columns along a shallow canopy and three stone figures on the roof. Maria and Joseph quickly walked inside while Bess and Jerome hovered at the door.

Along with a simple water pump at one end behind a counter, the large room inside Sherborne Spa was half filled with plants which were used as specimens in the botanical lectures given in the building. A telescope and other instruments were assembled at the other end of the room. Maria led Joseph behind some large plants, stopped and looked at him up and down. His green tweed coat was ripped at the elbows and shoulders, his once white shirt was soiled by dirt and dried blood. He had hopelessly tried to tie a neat collar but it was ripped and creased. She stared at his face where blood congealed on his upper lip, his eyes were downcast again.

Maria breathed quickly and then sighed, 'Now, tell me Joseph. What on earth has been going on? Did you send this note about calling off our betrothal; after all we have been through? What on earth has happened to you?' She quickly removed the letter from her reticule and thrust it into his hands; Joseph frowned, quickly read it, and then looked searchingly into her eyes.

'My dearest Maria, I did not send this note.' His voice was quiet and rasping, he screwed the paper up and shook his head. 'This is not my hand. I did not write this note dearest; you must know that it is not my fault that I have acted in so strange a manner towards you.'

Maria shook her head and grabbed the note from his hand, unscrewed it and held it up. 'So, who did write this note?'

Joseph pressed his hands together in desperation, 'I do not know, but it is probably the same person or persons who have done this to me.' He looked down at his coat and touched his lip.

Maria shook her head in disbelief, 'Of course Mr Hayne, of course, you have clearly been through an ordeal, but I need an explanation.'

Joseph nodded and held his hand to his forehead. 'I will try to remember it all... I was at the races... I went with a fellow called Thomas Jameson who plied me with liquor.' He paused to narrow his eyes. 'I really don't think he had any hand in it...but... I was in such a beastly state of intoxication that I knew not what I did; all I remember is being bundled into a coach which sped off at haste.' He turned away suddenly, embarrassed.

'When the journey finally came to an end I was thrown out of the carriage and taken to a little room. I was tussled up with a sack over my head and I lost all sense of time and didn't know where I was...I...I have only just made my escape. It took me an hour to get back to Cheltenham and I had nothing on me, my captors took everything. I managed to hail a coach with the promise that they would be reimbursed on our return to town.' Joseph looked at Maria imploringly.

Maria, who had put her hand to her mouth while she

listening, now removed it. 'And what of these captors? Did you hear any of them speak? Who would do this to you?' She thought for a moment and narrowed her eyes, 'Was Colonel Buckley present at the races?'

Joseph sighed and his shoulders dropped. 'Yes, Buckley was there with his gloating entourage. He could have enlisted them to help him with this scheme. Whoever did this was trying to prevent our marriage!' Joseph gestured to the note. 'Oh, I only just managed to escape.' Clasping Maria's hands, Joseph pleaded, 'My dear, this marriage must proceed as soon as possible!'

Maria shook her head but kept her hands in his. 'All of this will just add to the scandal already being gossiped about. Oh, it's just awful Joseph, and I want it all to end. Who would do this to you? To us? I can only think of one person!'

Joseph now regained his composure and put his hands gently on Maria's shoulders. 'I have my suspicions of course. And I have had some friends give their unwanted counsel on the subject of our marriage, but I will not be swayed in this matter. And neither should you, my dearest Maria. Please, let us be reconciled. Our marriage should take place as soon as possible.'

She looked at him steadily, 'You have tried to understand me and my situation. This was not your fault, but you must be careful in this town. Your friends will think the same as what many others think of me, but I am ready to be a wife. You have proved to me that you are kind… and… this is what I want.'

Maria rested her head on Joseph's torn coat and closed her eyes. She felt ashamed but mainly tired of the drama surrounding her name. If this man had run to her after such an ordeal, then surely he would be there for her in the future. She could hope for a life where she wasn't subject to every local gossip. An easy target for newspaper caricature. She had had enough.

Maria shook herself free and looked up at him again. 'Yes,

yes, as soon as possible.' She sighed as he took her in his arms and kissed her tenderly on the forehead.

Maria suddenly pulled herself away from him again, 'But your reputation? Surely the kidnapper was someone who seeks to prevent this marriage and stand in the way of our happiness? Not only are you risking your reputation, but you have offered to protect me and my children. I cannot ask you for anything more. If you would like some time to reconsider?'

Joseph looked into her eyes, 'No, dearest Maria! My mind is made up and we must be married as soon as possible. I am resolved to sacrifice friends to affection; I cannot, will not lose you.' They looked into each other's eyes and held a long reassuring kiss.

Chapter 21

Following the influx of visitors for the Cheltenham Races, the town had returned to near normality apart from talk of the two scandals. The upcoming public inquest concerning the reverend and the now well-known kidnapping of Joseph Hayne and the rumoured involvement of the notorious Colonel Buckley were all anyone talked about, from the servant classes to the Lords and Ladies visiting the spas. Both were widely surmised upon, reported in the local press, and diarised in publications nationwide.

The public inquest into the reverend's case was to be held in the Clarence Hotel, a newly built establishment to the north of the town. In the weeks since the gruesome delivery, the case had been investigated by the coroner, publicly sifted through, and large rewards were offered for the discovery of any person or persons who had been connected with the act. The reverend had kept to his normal routines but taken his carriage to church instead of his walks. An air of solemnity had held dominance over his household, despite the best efforts of Elizabeth to reassure her husband and the maids. The children, remaining unaware of the incident, had noticed a change in atmosphere and followed their mother's lead in trying to lift spirits. They sang hymns to their father and hugged him when he looked downcast.

The day of the inquest came and a large, long room in the hotel had been set out for the court. A raised wooden platform had been installed at one end with a desk in the centre, at which the elderly coroner with grey hair and silver glasses sat beside a simple wooden gavel and a set of notes. Beside him sat a clerk and in front of the platform there were twenty men of the town who had been drafted in as a jury. Behind the jury sat the reverend and Elizabeth with Harriet and Sarah beside them. The rest of the room was open to the public, and every seat was taken with standing room only at the back. Reporters leafed through pages of notebooks as people jostled to get inside before the doors to the room were shut and a silence descended on the court.

The coroner cleared his throat and peered over his glasses, 'We sit at this inquest today to hear the case involving the delivery of a deceased child to the Reverend Francis Cole's home on the night of 5th July past.' Reporters scribbled in their notepads and the crowd packed into the back of the room murmured while those seated shifted and settled in their seats.

The coroner continued, 'Beyond the fact that the basket, with every appearance of a fish basket, had been booked in London at the Great Western Station, nothing has transpired that could lead to the discovery of the culprit or culprits. Nearly £1,000 first to last has been offered by the parish officers, by the magistrates and by the reverend himself, but all in vain.'

The reporters scribbled more, and the crowd murmured again, many shook their heads. One man called out from the back, 'We have a good idea who was behind it all!'

The coroner glanced up quickly, frowned at the man and then banged his gavel onto its block. 'I will continue with reading out the facts as written down by the reverend and other witnesses.' He cleared his throat again and picked up his notes, 'And the facts are, that the basket containing the deceased child was received by the parlour maid Sarah Doleman on the evening of 5th July past at Lansdown House. The basket was then taken to the Reverend Cole by the cook Harriet Blant. After the discovery of the contents, the reverend and his staff stored the basket with the infant inside in his basement and then alerted the constable and the magistrates the following morning.'

There was more murmuring and the cook and parlour maid looked at each other solemnly before the coroner continued, 'The body was taken to the workhouse by the constable and then moved to the mortuary for medical examination. It was found that the infant died of natural causes and the child was subsequently buried. In his register the sexton has recorded "Buried – an infant from the workhouse. Name unknown."'

The coroner paused to write a note. The reverend looked at Elizabeth, his face pale. She clutched his hand as the coroner cleared his throat again and continued, 'After the journey from London, the basket and its contents were transferred to the Birmingham Railway. The delivery was then brought to the home of the reverend by a Mr Edward Artus. Mr Artus, an employee of the Birmingham Railway, has been vouched for and interviewed. He has no knowledge of who sent the delivery or what was in the basket.'

The crowd whispered and shuffled as the coroner scanned his notes. 'As we have not found the original sender of the delivery, we do not know to whom this infant belonged. We have not been able to ascertain if it was taken with or without the knowledge of the parent or parents. Nor do we know if money was exchanged in the course of this crime.'

The coroner put down his notes, brought down his gavel again and looked at the jury in front of him, 'So who has committed this terrible crime? The reverend has been investigated as a matter of course and is innocent of any wrongdoing and is a proven victim in this matter. However, we know that the Reverend Cole has a number of enemies who have made public objections to his Evangelical faith, his dominant leadership in Cheltenham, his opposition to the races, and to all activities that break the Sabbath. Those who sent the unfortunate child to Reverend Cole hoped to destroy his name and reputation but have failed to do so. I will now allow two statements to be read out to the court.' The coroner glanced over to the reverend. 'The first by the Reverend Cole. Please stand up and read your statement.' The coroner nodded and the reverend briefly looked at Elizabeth before standing up. His hands clasped a small piece of paper which he held before him. He slowly reached into his gown pocket for his gold spectacles and placed them on his nose. His usually loud and assured voice was now low and soft as he turned and faced the jury.

'Thank you, coroner for permitting me to speak. I wanted to say something here as my brethren know that I confront all of life's challenges head on.' His voice broke slightly. 'And this has certainly been a challenge. Firstly, it is all too clear that this atrocious and cruel insult to me and my family, inflicted evidently by base persons, was maliciously intended to damage my character.' The crowd murmured in sympathy. 'During the weeks prior to the incident, I have felt there were a number of attempts to disturb my peace and to break in upon the happiness of my domestic circle. I was followed on one evening before the incident and I believe there must have been a number of people involved, perhaps with one paying ringleader.' The crowd murmured even louder.

The reverend sighed, 'Whatever the intention of this plot, there can be little doubt that these attempts were designed to turn me from my path of duty in the evil spirit of personal malice and revenge.' The reverend paused again and looked about the room. 'But, despite this intention, it seems that this diabolical act has had the opposite effect. I have been able to entirely commit it into the hands of Almighty God and my duties abound, my resolve is stronger than before, and I have received many letters of support.'

The coroner raised his hand, nodding at the speaker. 'Reverend Cole, mark the result! I would like you to hear what our second speaker has to say before you conclude, if you please. You may remain standing.' The reverend frowned and looked around. 'Please rise Mr Fenton Hort, come to the front and read out your statement to the court.' The coroner nodded to a man who was now standing in the middle of the room.

Mr Hort was tall and wiry, and his neat grey hair matched a small grey moustache. Clutching a thick set of notes in his hands, he shuffled out of a row of seated onlookers and moved to a bench near the coroner, turned to the jury, then to the reverend, and bowed. His voice was deep and steady, 'Sirs, thank you for permitting me to speak today on behalf of five hundred and fifty householders of all sects and parties who have signed an address in support of the Reverend Cole.'

The reverend gasped and then bowed his head. Elizabeth looked up at her husband and beamed before turning to Harriet and Sarah to clasp their hands. The crowd broke into a chatter and several clapped before the coroner brought his gavel down again and pointed at Mr Hort who nodded earnestly and carried on, 'Since this incident, it is as if the whole population of Cheltenham has risen up indignantly as one man to protest against this brutal act. The reverend himself has received letters of kindness and sympathy, but we wanted to express our support more formally with the address I hold before me here today.'

Mr Hort held up his bundle of notes and handed them to the coroner who raised his eyebrows and began to leaf through the pages. Mr Hort continued, 'Sirs, this petition in support of our good reverend has been signed by hundreds: by persons of all ranks and classes, by dissenting ministers and clergymen, by magistrates, in fact, I know not any class of persons that is omitted. It may not be proven that this shameful act was attempted manifestly by those whose vices he condemns and whose sinful pleasures, especially of the racecourse, he has been successful in overthrowing. The culprits of this crime may never be found and brought to justice, but we believe the reverend should be placed in a position even higher and more influential than ever before occupied. This is why we support him here today.'

Mr Hort turned to address the reverend directly and raised his voice. 'It is also, I believe, the universal feeling of all by whom I am surrounded, that it was not against you Sir, as an individual, that the filthy outrage was directed, but that emanating from the dark spirit of evil, it has been launched against the pure religion of Jesus Christ of which you are the ever watchful and consistent champion.'

A cheer resounded in the room and a great clapping continued for five minutes. The coroner sat back in his seat and smiled, the jury gazed about in wonder, and the reverend sat down with his head in his hands. Elizabeth stared at her husband in joyous amazement. Harriet and Sarah looked at each other in disbelief.

The clapping gradually ceased as the reverend slowly got to his feet again. He put his hand on his heart and his voice was broken. 'My dear friends and parishioners, Mr Hort, I beg you to accept my heartfelt thanks for your kind and sympathetic address to me regarding the painful and revolting circumstances under which I have recently been placed. An expression of public feeling so general and spontaneous is more than sufficient to counterbalance my temporary pain which an insult so atrocious was calculated to create.'

There was another great clapping in the room before the chairman sat forward, banged his gavel, and addressed the jury. The twenty men filed out of the room dutifully and the crowd dispersed, but on hearing of the return of the jury within ten minutes, hurried back in again to pack the room. There was silence as the jury foreman stood up. The coroner placed his silver glasses on the end of his nose and peered at him.

'What is your verdict in this inquiry?'

The foreman, a middle-aged, heavy-set man with a beard, looked at the reverend, then to the crowd, and finally at the coroner. 'Sir, our verdict on the child's death is natural causes, but we would like to add our voices to the large petition of personal support for the Reverend Cole.' The man picked up a piece of paper which was lying on the bench in front of him. 'Here, we have all signed a declaration expressing our abhorrence at this incident.' The foreman passed it to the coroner who looked at it briefly and then placed it in front of him next to the petition.

'I consider this case closed.' The coroner brought his gavel down hard on the block and the whole room applauded the reverend who remained standing He wiped his eyes with a handkerchief and put his hands together in prayer.

Chapter 22

On the morning of her wedding day, Maria stood in front of the window at Deanswood overlooking the garden. It was early August and the willow tree's yellowed leaves rustled and the little swing enclosed in the leafy den drifted back and forth. The bride was wearing a cream gown with pink silk roses crafted on the breast and sleeves. The roses also encircled the dress just above the lace hem. She wore long cream silk gloves, and her hair was gathered in ringlets below a silver and pearl tiara.

The same pink silk roses adorned one side of Maria's hair. She raised a hand to her locket and held it as she gazed at the swing and smiled; her mind drifting to thoughts of her children as she imagined them playing among the branches and pushing each other on the swing. She took a deep breath and sighed. There had been no word from Buckley, and she no longer wanted to hear from him or see him again. She felt a surge of anger as she remembered his attempts to destroy her happiness with Joseph. Was he behind the kidnapping that day? It if wasn't him, he would certainly know men who would do it for him. Maria shook her head and focused on the day ahead – her marriage to a kind man who, she hoped, would welcome her children for them to be a family.

Maria shivered slightly despite the day being warm. She moved to her dressing table and looked in the mirror. Hetty had helped to dress and fix her hair, but as usual Maria had applied her own make-up. Her smooth, milky skin needed little embellishment; she had applied a small amount of rouge to her cheeks. Her large eyes needed no exaggeration and there was a mere dusting of white powder on the lids.

'Oh, you look beautiful Miss!' Hetty exclaimed as she entered the room. 'Your lawyer, Mr Gill is here with the marriage settlement. Your father and mother are with him now in the parlour.' The maid clasped her hands together and stared at her mistress. It was less than an hour until she would be picked up in her carriage and taken to the church.

'Thank you, dear Hetty. I will be down shortly.' She smiled as the maid left the room and Maria turned back to the mirror where she had one last look at herself. Married at last. A wave of relief washed over her, and she clasped her locket again. She opened it and kissed the little faces of Jane and Jack before closing it carefully. She then suddenly heard a call from below. It was her father.

'Maria!' her father called again. She reluctantly turned from her reflection as she heard unexpected voices downstairs. Moving slowly, as if she were in a dream, Maria walked out of her room to the top of the grand staircase which led down into the centre of the parlour. Maria clutched the wooden banisters as she carefully descended.

Standing in the parlour at the foot of the stairs, flanked by Mr Gill, her parents, and Hetty, was Joseph's solicitor Mr Bebb. All were silent as they looked up at the bride.

Mr Mount was for a moment struck by his daughter's beauty and beamed up at her. He then frowned slightly and turned to the solicitor, 'A Mr Bebb to see you, daughter. He wouldn't tell us what for.'

Maria walked slowly down the stairs into the parlour where Mr Bebb stood, his hat in both hands. He twisted it and looked awkwardly at the floor for a few moments before finally looking up at Maria who stood on the bottom step.

He nodded at her. His voice monotone, he said 'I have a

verbal message to announce to Miss Mount from Mr Hayne.'

Mrs Mount, who was standing behind her husband, tutted, 'Is there no letter or written message from him? Is he going to be late?'

Maria stood wide-eyed at the foot of the stairs and grabbed the banister.

Mr Bebb looked to Mrs Mount, 'I am afraid not madam.' He turned back to Maria, his head bowed slightly. 'Mr Hayne concludes that he has been divided between his concern for his reputation and for his love for you. Unfortunately, the loyalty to his reputation and friendships have come first in this instance.'

There was a gasp from Hetty and then a long, shocked silence before Mr Mount stepped towards the solicitor, 'Concludes? What on earth does that mean? Is he saying the marriage is off? But he promised me...' his voice tailed off, flustered.

'Father! Yes, that it what he means.' Maria stared at Mr Bebb who looked at the floor. 'Is this the only communication I am to receive from my defaulting bridegroom? Or is this another case of false pretences?'

Mr Bebb looked up, his voice now firm, 'Miss Mount, I am afraid this is not a false pretence. Mr Hayne is in quite a wretched state. He has gone into the country, to his seat at Kitson Hall in Staffordshire. His heart and thoughts are still with you, but the world is censorious, and my client had been divided between love for you and esteem for his friends and dread of their disapproval. He has decided to break off the match. You must regard his honour.' Mr Bebb bowed his head again and looked down at his hat.

Maria's hands were now clasped in front of her, 'His honour? And what of my reputation Mr Bebb, is that to be regarded?' she laughed manically. 'Do women have a say in their own reputation? Is this Mr Hayne's way of proving his love and regard for me?' Maria clutched the side of the banister and sank onto the bottom step. Hetty rushed to sit with her. Maria's parents remained standing and looked aghast at their daughter and then each other, while Mr Gill got out a notebook and started writing.

Maria started to cry, tears streamed down her face as she heaved a great sigh. 'Oh, how could he? My life, I should have known, my life.' She put her head in her hands. Hetty put her arms around her mistress who sobbed. The group stared and then Maria suddenly put her head up and put her arms out towards Mr Bebb. 'Tell him I will once more consent to see him.' She said desperately. 'Tell him I will forgive him this as he has forgiven me...'

Mr Bebb looked down at the actress with sympathy. 'Miss Mount, he did write a short note.' The solicitor reached into his briefcase, retrieved a folded sealed note, and handed it to her.

Maria took the note and unfolded it. She stopped crying, but her cheeks were wet, and her eyes swollen. She held the note in front of her and read it out, 'It says "Farewell forever. Hayne."' She screwed it up in her hand, put her head into her knees and sobbed.

Chapter 23

It was an unseasonably warm early September day when Elizabeth Cole walked into her husband's study carrying the *Cheltenham Chronicle*. The reverend was preparing for the opening of another new school; his reputation was restored and support for his causes from all ranks and classes had increased. The season in Cheltenham was coming to an end and the Cambray Theatre was less crowded since the sudden and much-discussed departure of Maria Mount, whose understudy had taken over for the last few performances of Romeo and Juliet.

Elizabeth stood in front of her husband's desk. The reverend looked up over his gold spectacles.

'Have you read the papers dear?' she placed them in front of him next to his notes.

The reverend frowned briefly and pushed them away, 'No, you know I never do. I would rather dedicate all of my time on my good works without any interference from gossip or scaremongering.'

Elizabeth gathered the papers back up and sat down in a chair opposite her husband. 'Well, there is something I would like to bring to your attention. I know you prefer not to get involved with the town gossip but this season we have very much been the centre of attention. Our news is no longer of interest thankfully, but the papers are still full of news about Maria Mount, the actress.'

The reverend nodded over his spectacles and listened. Elizabeth continued quickly, 'She is to sue Joseph Hayne for Breach of Promise, since he deserted her on the day of their wedding. The case is to be heard at the Court of the King's Bench no less. It has been quite the scandal since the lady left Cheltenham just over a week ago. She has not appeared at the last performances at the Cambray Theatre, and it has transpired that her parents have apparently gone missing with a substantial amount of money given by Hayne... and the whole town now knows of her previous involvement with Colonel Buckley and their estranged children. I must add that it is his name which has been most blackened by this.'

The reverend raised his hand at his wife, sighed and grimaced, 'Now Elizabeth, you know my views of the theatre and of that man Buckley and I pray that you don't get involved in this common gossip. If the actress has lost any chance of a financial settlement coming from the promised marriage to Mr Hayne, then the courts will see to it that this is rectified. We have nothing to do with it.' He waved his hand as if that was an end to the matter.

Elizabeth stood up and moved around the desk to stand next to her husband. 'But her story – her children, her reputation. I feel so sorry for her. Is there nothing we could do? She did not have a good start in life. The general feeling Francis, even from those in your flock, is that this woman has been wronged. You support the poor and downtrodden of this town, so surely you must see and forgive?'

The reverend sat back in his chair, rested his fingers together and looked up at Elizabeth. He was mildly annoyed at her continued persuasion, 'My dear, my reputation has already been challenged and I must focus on my causes.' The reverend nodded at his wife and picked up his notes to show her.

Elizabeth took the notes and placed them carefully back on the desk with the newspaper on top. The reverend briefly scanned a headline while she persevered. 'You can't pick and choose who you care for. Surely all God's subjects deserve your forgiveness and understanding at least?'

'Mostly, yes.' The reverend looked up and thought for a moment, he then grimaced. 'But, I detest that man Colonel Buckley. I won't utter it to anyone but you, but I suspect he had a hand in the despicable actions against me. I am not in the way of helping fallen actresses, especially those who have been associated with that man. I am sorry my dear, but I must draw a line.' The reverend picked up the papers and handed them back to his wife.

She persevered, 'And what of the mother of the poor wretch who was delivered to you?' Elizabeth now raised her voice. She leaned forward and put her hands on the reverend's shoulders and looked into his eyes. 'Did she have a choice? Did she know where her child went? We don't know if someone took her baby alive or dead, we shall never know. Oh, it's so horrible! I can't imagine ever being parted from our little ones! You must let me help her or allow me the freedom of sending a note of support.'

The reverend sighed and sat back. Their gaze continued to meet. He sighed again but eventually smiled, 'You are a most remarkable and good woman. This is why I love you so. When is the case to be heard? Of course, you can send a note of support.'

Elizabeth clasped her hands together and smiled, 'And perhaps when this is all over, we could offer her support to get her children back? I know it is unconventional, but with our influence and a letter of reference, she would be able to return to the town with her head held high. You know how it feels to have everybody talking about you, and how wonderful it was to receive the petition of support. Will you entrust me to do the same for Maria Mount?'

The reverend shook his head but smiled again. 'We have certainly seen it all this season. I do not care about scandal anymore, I only care about doing the right thing and I acknowledge that you have helped guide me to do that.' He looked at his wife lovingly and nodded. 'I will leave it in your capable hands my dear. Now, if you please, I must return to my notes.'

Elizabeth nodded, walked out of the room, and called for Sarah. She would begin by visiting The Jar and Pineapple at once to request Mr Bonfils' support. She was sure he would be the first to sign the petition in support of Maria Mount.

Chapter 24

Lady Croft reclined in her chaise longue in the drawing room of her home at Virginia Water. Lord Croft stood at the bay window, his eyes fixed on the wide curved driveway. Their grand villa sat in extensive grounds on a slight hill. Its slope descended to a beautiful tree-lined lake, beyond which were fields to one side and Cheltenham's new 'The Park' development to the other. The estate matched the ambitious plans of Pittville and already a number of houses had been built around a large teardrop shaded drive, Virginia Water being the first of them.

Lord Croft turned towards the room.

'Stay looking out there dear,' Lady Croft waved at her husband. 'I don't want to miss it. It must be coming soon. It's never this late.' Over the past few weeks Lady Croft had eagerly waited for the newspapers every morning and then proceeded to relate to her husband every article of news that the morning papers had supplied her with.

Lord Croft turned from the window, 'Gertrude, you've been making me do this every day. It's getting rather tiresome.' He sat down into an armchair nestled in the alcove of the bay window and picked up the previous day's copy of the *Cheltenham Chronicle* from a polished walnut table next to him.

Lady Croft sighed heavily and sat up. 'But I need to find out all the gossip from London. There was hardly anything on it yesterday even though the case against Mr Hayne is being heard tomorrow. Surely, they know their readership? Where is our delivery?'

Lord Croft was scanning the pages of yesterday's newspaper. 'Of course dear, but nothing much can be reported of a case until it is heard. It will be dealing with facts, while you especially deal rather more in opinion.' Lord Croft raised an eyebrow and paused as his wife failed to rise to his comment. Lady Croft had now stood up and began to pace the room. Her green morning tea gown swished around her as she moved jerkily.

Suddenly, the front doorbell sounded and moments later, there was a knock at the drawing room door. Lady Croft bounded over, grabbed the door handle, and greeted the butler who, before he could say anything, had the morning papers whisked from his gloved hands.

'Thank you, Simkins,' she nodded at the man. The butler's face remained impassive as he turned and walked out of the room. Lady Croft stood still as she opened the paper and sifted quickly through the pages. 'I see... there is the notice for the trial; a report here, rather small...just announcing the case tomorrow. Hayne is being represented by a Wilfred Scarlet.'

Lord Croft looked up, 'Ah, Wilfred Scarlet, well, he'll help. I always thought that Mr Hayne was such a naive young man.'

'Oh, and this!' Lady Croft raised her voice into a near screech. 'Let me read this my dear! My goodness, it is a letter from Joseph Hayne himself! Not only does he cause a sensation in our town, but he has written a letter to absolve himself of any blame!'

'A letter?' exclaimed Lord Croft. 'Really, of all the cowardly things...'

'I shall read it out my dear, now listen.' Holding the paper aloft, Lady Croft walked over and stood next to her husband. She leaned over his chair, moved the paper in front of him and pointed to a large advert which covered a whole page. She cleared her throat but her voice was shrill. 'It is titled,

"Mr Hayne and Miss Mount – a letter To the Editor of the Morning Post."'

'Hayne writes, "I felt something was due to truth, the notice taken in your paper of this morning, compels me, reluctantly, to put the public in possession of facts which I think will justify my conduct. I was not aware when I made a proposal to Miss Mount, that she had ever been under the protection of Colonel Buckley – her father and mother having always upheld her to be a paragon of virtue, and had not Colonel Buckley owned her having had children by him, I should have been in ignorance of the facts until too late to retrieve my happiness."' There was a pause as Lord Croft twisted his head to look at his wife, his eyebrows raised.

She continued, "'In anticipating the defence I have at the approaching trial – Mr Mount borrowed the sum of one thousand one hundred and fifty pounds from me, but I understand that the fear of being called upon to return it has induced him to make a continental tour. The mention of the above facts will I trust induce the public to suspend their further opinion until the appeal made to the Court of the King's Bench is decided. And in thus intruding upon their notice, I cannot but congratulate myself at my escape."'

Lady Croft dropped the paper onto her husband's lap and stood open-mouthed, 'So he is trying to push the responsibility for ending the engagement onto Maria?'

Lord Croft now scanned the letter, 'Well, what a fellow. Yes, he is asserting that he had not known of Maria's previous liaison with Buckley, or of the children, even though he had renewed his offer of marriage after he was fully apprised of their existence.'

Lady Croft tutted and grabbed the paper, 'Oh my, I do hope the court concludes in her favour. Fancy publishing a letter to ease one's conscience.' She paced the room and looked searchingly at her husband. 'I presume he has gone from Cheltenham now? And what of William, have you seen him?'

Lord Croft sighed. 'No, I haven't seen Buckley, but I've seen Craven at The Club; he looked very grave – probably sick to the back teeth of people talking about his brother.'

'Perhaps we should invite him here?' Lady Croft dashed towards her writing chest in the middle of the room.

Lord Croft put his hand up. 'I think, for the moment, it is best to let matters settle dear. Yes, Mr Hayne has returned to his Staffordshire seat, and I presume will be in London for the trial.' Lord Croft shook his head. 'He didn't know what he was getting into at all, did he?'

'Oh, he deserves everything he gets, the foolish young man. And what of his investment in the Pittville Estates? I heard he invested quite a considerable sum.'

Lord Croft laughed and shook his head, 'My dear, this is really none of our concern. Just feel safe in the knowledge that we wisely invested and bought our property here in The Park. I hear the plans for the Pittville zoological garden plans have stalled because, as we know, there are plans for a similar scheme here. The whole thing was embraced with too much eagerness, I feel. They sold 600 shares in the end and chose a site, but the Pittville development is losing money.'

Lady Croft moved towards him and flapped her arms, 'Oh, it sounds like quite a farce my dear. I don't think you should get involved?'

Lord Croft rubbed his chin. 'Well, I think with two plans – if they can't come to an agreement both will fail. Perhaps the speculative bubble will burst? I often wonder whether these men do it for the good of Cheltenham or to further their own commercial interests. So Hayne will lose his money. Not only did he invest unwisely in a future bride, but his business interests have failed and his reputation, here in Cheltenham at least, has been ruined.'

Lady Croft tutted again and sat back on her chaise lounge, 'Oh come, these are the chances gentlemen of breeding can make though, aren't they husband? Us gentlewomen must put up with your choices and make the best of it.'

'I hope you're not suggesting that you've made a bad choice, are you Gertrude?'

'I made the best choice of all. I wouldn't dream of doing without you.'

The couple smiled at each other and then Lord Croft tipped his head back into his reading of yesterday's paper while his wife reread Mr Hayne's letter through twice.

Chapter 25

German Cottage was a large villa on the outskirts of Cheltenham where Colonel William Buckley had enjoyed entertaining the great, good, and notorious of the town for over twenty years. Apart from their family seat at Buckley Castle, the Buckley's owned a large number of estates throughout the county which the family could reside in or simply use whenever they felt the desire. An unshaven Buckley stood alone in his grand drawing room by a blazing fire in the hearth. He surveyed the room which was rather sparse as its owner spent little time considering furnishings and decoration. Two large worn sofas sat in the middle of the room and two armchairs with a table in between were placed on the side. A number of family portraits adorned the walls and a stuffed stag's head peered imposingly above the door.

The sound of a carriage outside caused Buckley to move to the window. He looked out at the circular driveway now covered by soggy autumn leaves. His brother Craven stepped out of his modest black fly.

'Hmm, what he is here for?' Buckley mumbled to himself. Craven had his usual earnest look on his face as he strode to the front door. Buckley poured himself a drink from a decanter on the table and returned to the window before Craven shortly entered the drawing room with a maid following and curtsying behind.

'Craven.' Buckley turned, swigged his drink in one, and frowned.

'William.' His brother stood in the middle of the room, removed his gloves, and the pair looked at each other for a moment before Buckley waved off the maid and beckoned Craven to a seat.

'I will remain standing William, as I visit on a matter of some importance, and I don't expect to be here long.' Craven bowed his head slightly, put his gloves on an arm of one of the sofas and briefly stretched out his hands and examined his fingernails with forced calm.

'Oh, right.' Buckley gave a high laugh. 'You're not going to sit with your brother and have...'

'William!' Craven interrupted. 'This is no time for jest or for your manipulations. Have you any idea of the seriousness of what you have done?' his hands now stretched out from his sides in an appeal.

Buckley moved closer to his brother and raised his voice, pointing a finger at him and then at himself. 'What have I done? What have I done brother? Merely steered some innocent away from a scheming mistress of mine. She was mine. Miss Mount belonged to me and no one else. She was under my protection.'

'Yours!' Craven was now shouting as his face became increasingly redder. 'Don't be ridiculous man. She was never yours as you didn't do the honourable thing and marry the girl!' He stepped towards Buckley and pointed at him. The pair were now standing in the middle of the room a few feet away from each other, 'You're no better than father. You of all of us should have learned that it doesn't pay to keep secrets and act dishonourably. This Breach of Promise case is all anyone is talking about.'

'That case has nothing to do with me!' Buckley shouted. 'I am...'

'Are you deluded man?' Craven shouted over his brother as

he moved even closer. He brought his finger close to Buckley's face and then jabbed it towards the window. 'The whole town has been following it and knows of your involvement. Even the Attorney-General mentioned you by name.'

There was a pause as Buckley stumbled back and sank down into one of the armchairs. He looked at his brother and rolled his eyes.

Craven scowled at him, his voice stern, 'Can you not even take that seriously? It was reported that the Attorney-General himself remarked how he could not trust himself in using language he thought sufficient to express his detestation of Colonel Buckley's conduct, he said that yes!' Craven raised his eyes to the ceiling, 'You are a gambler of the worst kind. One who had played without any concern for human consequences.'

Buckley stared at his brother in shock as he now continued in a quieter voice, 'The case is over now. Mr Hayne's lawyer tried to accuse Miss Mount of witchery and seduction, but the jury came back in her favour. She was awarded damages of three thousand pounds, considerably less than her suit but I think that will be eaten up by the lawyers.'

'And me?' Buckley now stood up and moved towards his brother. 'Was there anything more said about me?'

Craven shook his head in disbelief. 'You're the most self-centred fellow I have ever encountered. No, there was nothing else about you. But it's you who is being talked about in Cheltenham. Mr Mount too of course, he's come out worst of all as his actions have been found out. Apparently Mr Hayne isn't the first to be swindled out of money from him and people are horrified about how he treated Miss Mount with the dirtiest selfishness.'

Buckley laughed, 'Joseph Peagreen Hayne is a fop who did not know his own mind from one day to another.'

'No matter brother! I come to speak about you today.' Craven held his hand to his head in exasperation. 'I have stood by you for many a year, even in my esteemed position. I have been advised many times to put you aside and to deal with your behaviour, and I have always ignored that advice. But this time, William, I will not defend you. I *cannot* defend you. This time William, I am strongly advising you to leave the county.'

Craven took a deep breath.

'William, I come to you today to speak with you about a matter far more severe than this misadventure involving Hayne and Miss Mount. I am afraid your name has been linked with a far graver incident.' Craven stared back at his brother who stood silently for a moment and then started to pace the room, his eyes now darting from one thing to another and his hand on his forehead. Craven stood and watched him until finally Buckley sat back down on the armchair.

'You do know which incident I talk about?' Craven's voice had now returned to its normal level.

'No, I don't.' Buckley shook his head like a sarcastic school-boy and rolled his eyes again.

Craven looked at him steadily. 'The incident involving the Reverend Cole. You know what I am talking about as your name has been linked with it. If you were behind this abominable act, then you should confess.'

'I had nothing to do with it.' Buckley sat back in the seat and lifted his head defiantly.

Craven's voice shook as he looked steadily at his brother, 'The child, William! The poor, dead infant who was delivered to the reverend's door like a piece of meat!'

'Me?' Buckley implored. 'Do you really think I was behind that?'

Craven shook his head sadly, 'Yes, brother, I'm afraid to say, I do. I believe that you would have done that. Your obsession with the man...' he reached into his jacket pocket and produced a small, dirty note.

'I have this note. It was handed to me by one of your associates... it is instructions for a delivery...I know your hand-writing William...' Craven's voice tailed off and he sighed as Buckley now put his head in his hands.

Craven spoke softly. 'William you must leave. For your sake and mine. If I can't make you do it then it will be pitchforks at the door I tell you, there is such strength of feeling. And... I must tell you that I intend to take our family title as I am the one who can rightfully... claim it.' Craven's voice faltered.

Buckley looked up at his younger brother and stared. 'What? But it is rightfully mine; I am the eldest! You have no right!' He suddenly jumped up at Craven in rage. His arm raised and his fist clenched, Buckley charged as his brother reeled in horror and quickly ducked before the blow could land. Buckley instead crashed forward and hit a sofa, he knelt on the floor and pounded the cushions violently with both hands. Craven stood behind him and watched as his brother finally sank to the floor and sobbed.

Craven shook his head as he looked down at his older brother. 'William, in the eyes of the law, the title is rightfully mine. Now let this be an end to your quest. It is for your own good... and mine. For most of my life I have looked up to you. I always knew you were arrogant and self-centred, but with that came a drive; a determination: something which has inspired me to gain my position and so I still love you for all you have taught me, despite all that you have done. But now I see.' He shook his head mournfully as Buckley looked up at him now with tears streaming down his face.

Craven spoke still softer, 'I see that your arrogance is just a front. You are weak, William. Your quest to take the title has overshadowed everything else in your life. What you are suspected of being behind, but will not admit to, is evil. I don't expect you to admit to it... but I know you were behind it. Like so many other incidents you have been behind. You cannot hold your head up in this town any longer William.' He shook his head again. 'And it will take me a long time to move on from the scandal.'

Buckley lifted his head; his eyes searched Craven's face for a moment and then he looked down again. His hands covered his eyes and head as his sobbing increased into loud moans.

'The child was already dead when I... I hired a man to... I never meant to hurt Miss Mount... our children.'

Craven stood for a while on the same spot looking at Buckley with a mixture of pity and disgust before putting his gloves back on, turning around and walking out into the fresh autumn air.

Cheltenham May 1835

Chapter 26

The new season had started with unusually warm weather. A number of recently opened smaller spas had been established in Cheltenham by those still capitalising on the fashion for taking the waters. Some had deserted the town in favour of the new fad of sea bathing, but as a resort which still attracted the important families during the season, Cheltenham's promenades and walks remained busy.

The town was especially busy as there was an overruling need to be present to witness the return of Maria Mount to the Cambray Theatre. Her absence from the stage since the previous season was all anyone had talked about throughout winter. Whether the scheming actress, the naive speculator, or the devious lover was to blame was a popular topic of debate at society dinner parties, and often these debates devolved into bitter arguments. Many a husband and wife had retired to bed not speaking due to their differing views on the scandal of last season. However, despite the debate, Maria's reputation had been all but restored. The public felt she was to be pitied more than blamed. Brought up by such detestably mean parents, without protection, exposed to temptation at every turn, the town felt she was due a benefit in her honour.

In this first week of the season, Maria had arrived in

Cheltenham. Her children, their nanny and her staff had accompanied her and installed themselves at Deanswood, which had been thoroughly spring cleaned and filled with new clothes and toys. Maria's heart was full as she watched her little children run into the garden for the first time. She had allowed them to discover it themselves and smiled and waved at them as they ran to the swing in the huge weeping willow. Maria laughed as they took turns to push each other higher and higher, up through the sweeping branches. Any trace of Mr and Mrs Mount's belongings had been removed. Maria had heard nothing from her parents since their disappearance and she no longer cared where they were. Hearing of Joseph's deal with her father had not surprised her, nor had Colonel Buckley's lack of contest for the custody of their children. She felt the same way about him as she did for her parents: a mixture of pity and disgust.

Maria and Hetty had settled her children into their little wooden beds in the nursery before the actress had departed for the evening's first performance at Cambray Theatre. The theatre was packed. In fact, it was the fullest house of any season with audiences assembled, not for the performance of The Belle's Stratagem, but for the triumphant reappearance of Miss Mount. For the past weeks, every seat in the boxes, dress circle, first circle and pit were engaged. Even part of the orchestra was moved to accommodate more visitors with guinea tickets, and before the rising of the curtain; the whole interior of the theatre was crowded almost to suffocation.

In one of the seats in the dress circle sat Elizabeth Cole. Some glanced over in shock at the sight of the reverend's wife at the theatre. 'Who is she with?' whispered some. 'She seems to be alone, or is that a friend next to her?' But most were too excited to see the lady about to appear on the stage to be interested. 'Good for her,' nodded a lady to her companion sitting opposite Elizabeth. 'If she wants to visit the theatre, then she should. Supporting Maria Mount doesn't mean she can't also support the good works of the reverend.'

The curtain lifted and during the first scenes of the performance little else was heard other than the whispering and shuffling of the audience. Then, after what seemed like a long wait, there was a sudden stillness and quiet. Maria Mount appeared. A loud burst of applause rose throughout the audience. It began in the pit, then spread to the boxes and throughout the theatre as patrons stood to join the applause, removing their hats, or producing handkerchiefs to wave in support and appreciation. Many even wept.

Maria stood in the middle of the stage. She wore a simple white gown; her raven hair fell loosely, and her eyes were wide. She took a faltering step to the front of the stage and began to cry. It was clear throughout the play that many scenes had been inspired by Miss Mount's own peculiar situation the year prior. When the actress encountered a suitor, the audience held its breath as a buck-sure male lured her character over to him on a platform, looked her up and down and asked, 'What is your fortune, my pretty maid?'

Maria looked up at him on the platform, 'My face is my fortune, sir.'

At these words, the audience burst into another rapturous applause which equalled her entrance.

'Then I'll not marry you, my pretty maid.'

Maria replied with her nose in the air and a wave of her hand, 'There's nobody asking you, Sir.'

The audience erupted into applause again for a full five minutes and Maria bowed to the audience and beamed with pride.

Backstage after the performance, Maria looked into her dressing room mirror. She no longer wore her locket as she knew she would see her children on her return from the theatre every day. She smiled to herself as she removed the make-up from her face.

There was a knock at the door and her assistant peered in. 'A Mrs Cole to see you, Miss Mount.'

Maria laughed, 'Oh, please allow her in.' The actress sat wide-eyed as the reverend's wife entered the room. Her outfit of a high-buttoned grey coat and matching grey hat was quite incongruous to the red dressing room. She glanced at the wardrobe in the corner, its lavish and colourful costumes spilling out over the floor. She stood awkwardly for a moment and looked around in amazement. The cosy glow of the gas lights softened her nerves and she smiled.

'Miss Mount, I do hope you remember me. We met in The Jar and Pineapple last season. I have been following your distressing case and I have been waiting for you to return to Cheltenham.'

Maria smiled, 'Of course I remember you. Please, call me Maria.' She paused. 'You had your daughter with you, and I remember thinking you were quite bold to be making plans with Mr Bonfils - are you allowed to come here to see me here?'

'My husband is aware, yes. You may know of our own scandal last year. He has softened in some ways and trusts me to follow the right course. If I may call you Maria, then you must call me Elizabeth.' She stepped forward to shake Maria's hand. In her other hand she held a rolled-up scroll which she passed to the actress. 'I wanted to give you this.'

Maria took the scroll, stared at it, and then opened it slowly. She quickly scanned the text, 'A petition of support for Miss Maria Mount.' The actress stared at the list of names both signed and printed. She held her heart and looked at Elizabeth, her face flushed.

'Oh my goodness! How unexpected. Many of these names are people who I would never believe would support me!'

'You know there has been an outpouring of support for you Miss Mount... Maria. I wanted to present you with evidence of support for you here in Cheltenham.'

Maria looked down at the scroll again and wiped away a tear. 'This means so much to me, Elizabeth. Thank you.' The actress put her hand to her heart and Elizabeth smiled.

'It is my pleasure to bring you this Maria. You must also know that Mr Bonfils played a large part in obtaining signatures. He had a petition to sign in The Jar and Pineapple.'

Maria now stood up and clapped her hands in delight. 'Oh yes, I haven't been back yet. I must visit to thank him.' She paused. 'My children are now here with me in Cheltenham. I would be delighted to introduce them to yours – I believe they are of a similar age. Perhaps we could meet soon at The Jar and Pineapple?' Maria looked quizzically at Elizabeth who beamed.

'Your children, they are here in Cheltenham? Well, yes, of course. One day, I may even convince my husband to join me. But for now, let us meet there!'

'Yes, I have gained custody. Our MP, Craven had a hand in it. I'm just so very happy.' Maria beamed and stepped towards Elizabeth to hold her hands. For a moment she looked at the reverend's wife and shook her head in wonder. Her disbelief in her own self-worth after all Buckley's promises and Hayne's abandonment now seemed like a wound being healed. Helped by this woman and welcomed back by so many. She felt so grateful to her and to Mr Bonfils and all those in Cheltenham who so openly supported her. She wiped away a tear as she bowed to Elizabeth.

'Thank you my dear. I look forward to our next meeting.'

Chapter 27

Mr Bonfils' creations gained popularity in Cheltenham as his reputation extended far and wide, with visitors coming from all over the county and beyond to sample his famous ices. His continued charity and support of the reverend's causes had afforded him a unique place in the town.

Since the departure of the blackened Colonel William Buckley, only the hardened racegoers unafraid of sullying their reputation were publicly supporting the event this season. The reverend had already launched a protest from the pulpit and there followed a promise to use every legal means to put down and discourage the races. But although the opposition was vigorous and determined, the supporters of the races were equally anxious to hold their own and keep up their favourite sport. No doubt, many visitors from out of town would attend, even though esteemed members of Cheltenham society did not wish to be associated. With the MP Craven Buckley now outwardly supporting the reverend's rally against the sport, many predicted a less successful season than before.

The theatres and other attractions, however, were ever popular and the reverend still had a long way to go in persuading the people to simply observe the Lord and concentrate on religious and educational pursuits. Some, Elizabeth Cole included, saw the need for some pleasurable 'rewards' for the hard-working men and women of the town, and she had striven to build up a firm friendship with Mr Bonfils, who not only dedicated his time to businesses but in giving back some of his healthy profits to help fund the reverend's schools.

It was a warm May day when Elizabeth returned with her children to The Jar and Pineapple. She had become bolder after visiting the theatre, and today Elizabeth had simply informed her husband of her intention to visit the shop, rather than asking his permission. Mr Bonfils was busy in the backroom, the smell of roses drifted through, and Elizabeth closed her eyes for a moment. The sound of her children clinking their spoons against the sides of their glass bowls was interrupted by the bell tinkling on the door and the entrance of Maria.

The actress's children were either side of her and stood wide-eyed as they looked around the sweet emporium. Their mother bowed down to speak to them and stroked their hair gently before looking up. Elizabeth stood up and there was a moment between the two ladies when they simply stared at each other and smiled. Mr Bonfils broke the spell as he started to sing, his rich voice echoing from within the backroom. Both Maria and Elizabeth laughed and then suddenly rushed towards each other and clasped each other's hands. Maria's children looked at their mother in wonder. Mr Bonfils heard the arrival of his most famous visitor, bounded out of the kitchen, and busied himself with setting up another table next to Elizabeth's.

Once sat down with ices ordered and sweets distributed to the children, Maria and Elizabeth looked at each other again and laughed. The children babbled and a dish of sweets were placed on the table. Isobel and Jane carefully shared out the delights as Jack and Clarence eagerly waited in obedience. Once they had their allocation, each child savoured the sweets differently. The girls taking time to suck the pleasurable goodies, while Clarence placed his in a line and Jack scoffed the lot quickly one after another.

Maria looked at them all fondly for a moment. She bent down to her daughter and put her ear to the girl's lips and laughed before looking back up at Elizabeth. She thought of all she had been through to reach this point. The people who had left, but none of it mattered, as the two people she loved most in the world were now here. She looked across at her new friend and said gently, 'This is all I wanted.'

Elizabeth reached over the table and held Maria's hand. Her voice was soft, 'I know.'

Historical Notes –
The Jar and Pineapple

Cheltenham is a fascinating place to research history as many of its stories have been forgotten. Perhaps this is because it only enjoyed a brief 'boom' when it was part of the society circuit. With the discovery of the spring waters in 1716, its repute only grew when Henry Skillicorne capitalised on the original well in 1738: enclosing it and planting walks and gardens. The Cheltenham waters continued to gain good reputation and in 1788, King George III visited. This set the seal on the town's reputation as a fashionable resort, and it soon surpassed Bath in its renown. In the early 1800s, the town continued to grow in population and there was a building boom. During the Regency era (officially 1811 to 1820 but unofficially 1795-1837) there were public and private well spas throughout the town.

By the time Queen Victoria came to the throne, the popularity of drinking spa waters had waned. A number of ambitious speculations were only half-built and soon Cheltenham's reputation as a place of health was surpassed by its reputation as a place of education with the building of schools and colleges.

The Cheltenham Races were hugely popular during the boom times as part of the 'pleasure' resort people flocked to. However, after the arrival of the formidable Reverend Francis Close in 1824, opposition to the sport mounted.

The Jar and Pineapple involves real Cheltenham events, places, and people, however there has been some degree of artistic licence. Extensive research has been carried out at the Cheltenham Local History Library and the Gloucestershire Archives. See below for details.

Places

The Cheltenham Racecourse: the existing site of the Cheltenham Racecourse at Prestbury Park is not its original. The races began in 1815 on Nottingham Hill - a smaller neighbour to Cleeve Hill - before moving to higher ground on Cleeve Hill in 1818. Following protests at the site in 1830 and the burning down of a grandstand, the races moved temporarily to Andoversford where a racecourse still exists today. The Cheltenham Races returned to town to be held at Prestbury Park, then were briefly back at Cleeve Hill. The races did not run for a number of years in the 1840s but were then reinstated at Prestbury Park where they remain today.

Old Prestbury Manor and Prestbury Park:the site of the manor on the furthest bend of the racecourse is a quiet spot where trees hang over a moat-like pond. In the reign of Elizabeth I, a splendid mansion stood at this site and the origins of the house go back 500 years before that. The pond we see today is all that is left of the moat. Of the house, not a stone remains. There is no record of a fire or other disaster, so what happened to deprive Prestbury of its own stately home?

Prestbury Park was a medieval deer park, and the Bishops of Hereford had a country residence at the moated site in Spring Lane. The Cravens, based successively in Berkshire and Warwickshire, then became lords of the manor of Prestbury and owned the land in and around the park, as well as the deeds and land transfer documents.

The manor had many owners but the main sources for the house's history are preserved in the papers of the

Chamberlayne and Craven families in the Gloucestershire Record Office. Also, excavation of the site in 1951 showed it had a large banquet hall with a chapel on the first floor and a separate kitchen building. Later improvements included a decorated plaster ceiling with pendants and an ornate stone fireplace with coloured tiles. The chapel became a living room, and the old-fashioned great hall was turned into a kitchen.

The manor suffered a stream of absent and careless owners with a number of lawsuits claiming ownership over the years.

Over the years it has had tenants and became a quarry for building materials. In 1762 Edmund Chamberlayne sold it to the current Lord Craven – two pieces of pasture ground being the site of the Manor of Prestbury.

Why did the bishops' manor house not survive? The answer must lie in Sir Thomas Chamberlayne's transfer of the manor lands to the Earl of Leicester. A fine house needs its surrounding land. The confusion over ownership must have hastened the house's decline.

The fields were leased in 1821 inc. by Prestbury yeoman Thomas Robinson. They seemed destined for an uneventful future. In 1823 however, Robinson signed an agreement with John David Kelly – secretary and agent of the gentlemen forming the committee for the purpose of erecting a Grandstand for the Cheltenham Races. The committee thereby acquired the use of three fields for one week in every year in either June or July. They would be entitled to the income from racing booths except that the farmer might erect a booth to charge for carriages.

St Mary's Minster Parish Church: the Minster is the only surviving medieval building in Cheltenham. It has been in continuous use for 850 years, though between 1859 and 1877 it was closed intermittently for repairs. Francis Close was incumbent at the church between 1826 and 1856. His bible and carrying case are still held in the vestry.

The Montpellier Gardens: developed as 'pleasure grounds' to compliment the Montpellier Pump Rooms.

Montpellier Pump Rooms: originally a wooden building erected by Henry Thompson in 1809, it was later rebuilt in stone in 1817. The dome was added later on by architect John Papworth.

Cambray Theatre: built by John Boles Watson around 1818. The theatre burned down in 1839. The description in this book is based on the Everyman Theatre which was built much later in 1891.

Pittville Pump Rooms: in the early 1820s, a banker named Joseph Pitt commissioned the architect, John Forbes, to design a pump room that was to act as the centrepiece to his vision of a town to rival Cheltenham - a town he would call Pittville. The foundation stone was laid on 4 May 1825 and the work completed in 1830.

Sherborne or Imperial Spa: founded in 1818 by local architects the Jearrad Brothers, the design was modelled on the Temple of Jupiter in Rome. Until the Sherborne Spa's opening, the Promenade, upon which the spa was situated, was a soggy, marshy track way. This was transformed into an attractive tree-lined avenue. The name was changed to Imperial Spa but by 1837, the spa was running out of water, so the building was dismantled and rebuilt further down the Promenade, just behind where the Neptune Fountain sits now.

The Well Walk: a 900-yard, tree-lined walk which led from the Royal Well (now under the Cheltenham Ladies' College) to the Parish Church of St. Mary's.

Montpellier Arcade: built in 1831-2. It was one of the first covered shopping areas in the country.

Imperial Fountain: an Italian marble fountain now installed on the Broadwalk, Cheltenham. Believed to have been looted from Italy during the Napoleonic Wars by the French and then captured by the British and sold to a Cheltenham solicitor. It is now on display on the Broadwalk within a little garden attached to the buildings.

Virginia Water: the first property at The Park estate. A lake was created from two brooks. It is now the site of a block of flats, but a small lake still exists.

People

Reverend Francis Close: incumbent at the Parish Church of St. Mary's from 1826-1856. His sermon 'The Evils of the Racecourse Exposed' was preached in the church in June 1827.

Close served as rector for thirty years, where he was a popular preacher and evangelical. He advocated for the creation of a training college for schoolteachers and opposed alcohol, tobacco, horse racing, and theatrical amusements. He was involved in the provision of new churches in Cheltenham. In 1856, he was nominated to be Dean of Carlisle Cathedral by the Prime Minister, Lord Palmerston, and the appointment was approved by the Queen. At the time of his resignation, he was the oldest of all deans in the Church of England. He died in Penzance the following year, on 12 December 1882, and was buried in Carlisle Cathedral.

Colonel William Berkeley 1st Earl FitzHardinge: a member of the aristocratic Berkeley family. Berkeley was the eldest son of Frederick Berkeley, 5th Earl of Berkeley and Mary Cole, daughter of William Cole. He had many siblings. Great uncertainty was raised about whether his parents had been officially married before his birth. William sought to prove his legitimacy in order to claim the Earldom following his father's death in 1810 and he applied to be summoned to the House of Lord as Earl of Berkeley. The Committee for Privileges decided that the Berkeley marriage of 1786 was "not then proved" and that the petitioner's claim was not made out. William received Berkeley Castle and the other estates by will, and on 2 July, after the adverse decision of the Lords Committee, he claimed a writ of summons as a Baron as Baron by tenure of Berkeley Castle. The claim was fully laid before the Committee for Privileges in 1828 and 1829, but the Lords gave no judgement on the case. The eldest son born after the 1797 Lambeth marriage of the fifth Earl, Thomas Moreton FitzHardinge Berkeley, became on the Earl's death in 1810 *de jure* 6th Earl of Berkeley — however, he refused to claim his right to the earldom. In 1831 William Berkeley was raised to the peerage as Baron Segrave, of Berkeley Castle in the County of Gloucester.

Berkeley was returned to parliament as one of two representatives for Gloucestershire in 1810 (succeeding his uncle Sir George Cranfield Berkeley), a seat he only held until 1811. He succeeded his father as Colonel of the Royal South Gloucestershire Light Infantry Militia in 1810 and commanded it until his death. In 1836 he was appointed Lord-Lieutenant of Gloucestershire, a post he retained until his death. In 1841 he was further honoured when he was made Earl FitzHardinge.

Berkeley never married. He had several mistresses, and in 1821 John Waterhouse succeeded in an action for "criminal conversation" (adultery) against him, being awarded £1000 damages at Gloucester Assizes over Berkeley's affair with Mrs Waterhouse. He died at Berkeley Castle, Gloucestershire, in October 1857, aged 70. The barony of Segrave and earldom of FitzHardinge died with him. The FitzHardinge title was revived in 1861 when his younger brother Maurice Berkeley was created Baron FitzHardinge.

Maria Mount: based on the real Maria Foote - an actress and mistress to William Berkeley who bore him two children.

In about 1816, actress Maria Foote, then aged about 17 or 18, was invited to perform at Cheltenham Theatre. She had already played Juliet and Miranda as well as many other roles, at her father's theatre in Plymouth and in Paris, but she was popular with audiences for her beauty rather than her talent.

During the season, the manager of the theatre told her that she had attracted the interest of Colonel William Fitzhardinge Berkeley, who wanted to take part in her 'benefit.' Before long, Berkeley and Foote had become lovers, with Berkeley promising marriage. There were obstacles to this: first and foremost, he was a notorious rake and liar; second, he was in the process of laying claim to his inheritance by trying to prove that his parents' marriage was legitimate.

She then became embroiled in a love triangle with William Berkeley and Joseph Hayne, but following Mr Hayne's retraction of his marriage offer, she had lost the chance of a financial settlement from the marriage. She decided to sue for breach of promise to marry, and her case was heard in the Court of King's Bench in December 1824. The jury retired for 15 minutes and came back with a verdict in Maria's favour and awarded her damages of £3,000.

Following the case, there was a public benefit in 1825 at Covent Garden Theatre. The house was packed, and she was given a rapturous reception. She continued to perform until 1831,when on 7th April she was married to the eccentric Charles Stanhope, eighth Earl of Harrington and Viscount Petersham. He was aged fifty-one and she aged thirty-three. They had one daughter; he died in 1851, and she, as Dowager Countess of Harrington, lived until 27 December 1867.

Joseph Pitt (1759–1842) was a British lawyer of humble origins who prospered as a property speculator, notably in Cheltenham, Gloucestershire, but also in Wiltshire, and who served as a Tory MP for Cricklade, Wiltshire 1812–1831. His name is commemorated in Pittville, Cheltenham, and his largest speculative development.

Joseph Hayne: described during the time as a 'rich foolish and dissipated young man about town', he was notoriously sued for breach of promise in 1824 by Maria Foote after he refused to marry her on the grounds of her relationship with Colonel William Berkeley. He was called, apparently by Berkeley, 'Pea-Green' Hayne due to a green coat he wore and was also known as 'the Silver Ball', a reference to his rival, Ball Hughes, 'the Golden Ball'. Hayne figures or is thought to figure in several satires in the period.

Craven Berkeley: first MP for Cheltenham after the Reform Act in 1832. Younger brother to William Berkeley. Whig/ Liberal. 1832-1847, 1848, 1852-55. Craven was first elected as MP for Cheltenham unopposed after the town won its own parliamentary representative for the first time in the Great Reform Act of 1832. He was re-elected in 1835 against token opposition from a Radical candidate. His election campaigns were boisterous affairs involving entertainment, marching bands decked out in his orange and green colours and several small riots.

Craven repeatedly crossed swords with 'the Pope of Cheltenham', the formidable evangelical Anglican and arch-Tory Francis Close. Craven certainly didn't share Close's disapproval of racing, theatre, and drink, especially on the Sabbath, and accused him of slander after Close called him 'an atheist, an infidel and a scoffer at religion'. Close must have felt vindicated when Craven later opposed Sunday trading restrictions and proposed an amendment to Sunday pub opening hours which would have removed the closing times.

Events

The Cheltenham Races: began on Nottingham Hill in 1815, they then moved to Cleeve Hill in 1818. The Reverend's sermon, 'The Evils of the Racecourse Exposed' in 1827 led to protests at race meetings. The grandstand on Cleeve Hill mysteriously burned down in 1830. Steeple chasing became established in nearby Andoversford from 1834 and moved to the present course in 1898.

Racing at Andoversford: despite flat racing having died a quiet death at Prestbury Park in the 1840s, Steeple chasing flourished a little further out of town on the present site of Andoversford Races, and here in 1834, the race known as the Grand Annual, was inaugurated. The Grand Annual, now one of the most fiercely competitive handicaps of the Festival, is a fixture of the Friday that also features the Cheltenham Gold Cup.

Sermons, Letters, and news stories: all taken from real accounts from the Reverend Francis Close's sermons, news extracts and a biographical account of his life. Breach of Promise case covered in news extracts and letters of the time.

This Diabolical Act incident: a deceased child was presented to Francis Close and there were at least two occasions when Close was accused of fathering illegitimate children.

The first case was brought before the magistrates and then dismissed. The Irish woman who accused Close returned to Ireland and confessed that the father was a drunken Cheltenham lawyer. The second incident occurred in Feb 1844 when Close was at the height of his powers as the perpetual curate of the parish church. A basket sent from Birmingham and apparently containing fish was delivered to his home at The Grange. It was received by the parlour maid Sarah Doleman and opened by the cook Harriet Blant. She immediately took it to Close in his study. The basket contained a few fish and a small black coffin containing the corpse of a dead boy aged about nine months. On it was a note reading 'Behold thy likeness.' Who had committed this terrible crime? Close had a number of enemies who objected to his Evangelical faith, his dominant leadership in Cheltenham, his opposition to the races, and to all activities that broke the Sabbath. He was opposed to Sunday travel and to trains bringing undesirables into Cheltenham. Those who sent the baby to Close hoped to destroy his name and reputation, but failed to do so as a public inquest held at the Clarence Hotel cleared his name and a petition of support was presented by local people.

Close later recorded the whole incident in his private journal.

Zoo Wars: in the autumn of 1836, two opposing companies fought to establish a zoological garden in the town. The sites at The Park and Pittville were mapped out, investors secured, and plans laid. The zoo projects were an ambitious and imaginative scheme, but due to insufficient funds and collaboration, the 'zoo war' marked the end of the building boom as neither of the proposals came to fruition and few animals were ever acquired.

Buns and Tea: Reverend Francis Close held an annual Buns and Tea event on the Well Walk for children who did not attend the Cheltenham Races.

Cheltenham Looker-On: a weekly society publication was a social and literary weekly periodical published in Cheltenham, England between 1833 and 1920. A lot of real events and descriptions in The Jar and Pineapple were taken from accounts at the time, including uniforms of the Montpellier Band, boats on the Pittville Lake, descriptions of the plants/cactus in Montpellier Spa, and the improvements to the Imperial Fountain and Montpellier Gardens.

Ice cream making in the Regency era: ice cream was a luxury during this time. There was no way of making ice artificially – it had to be harvested and stored which was easy enough if you had a large estate with lakes and ponds which would freeze in winter and staff to do the work. It was an expensive process: storing giant blocks of ice dug deeply enough underground to allow the ice to remain frozen during the summer months. Since ice cutting, transporting, and storing were laborious, this made the cost of ice very high so only the rich could consume ice cream. Flower flavours were common – violets, orange flowers, jasmine roses, and elderflowers. The vanilla bean, although appreciated for its agreeable flavour, did not rise in popularity until Victorian times.

Acknowledgements

James Sainty

Susan Oliver

Rachel Clements

Helena Fairfax

Heather Weyman

Printed in Great Britain
by Amazon